USE TO BE THE SWEETEST

NATIONAL BEST SELLING AUTHOR
Linette King

She Used to Be the Sweetest Girl
-Written By-
Linette King

Copyright © 2015 by True Glory Publications
Published by True Glory Publications
Join our Mailing List by texting TrueGlory to 95577

Facebook: **Author Linette King**

This novel is a work of fiction. Any resemblances to actual events, real people, living or dead, organizations, establishments or locales are products of the author's imagination. Other names, characters, places, and incidents are used fictitiously.

Cover Design:
Editor: Tamyra L. Griffin

All rights reserved. No part of this book may be used or reproduced in any form or by any means electronic or mechanical, including photocopying, recording or by information storage and retrieval system, without the written permission from the publisher and writer.

Because of the dynamic nature of the Internet, and Web addresses or links contained in this book may have changed since publication, and may no longer be valid. The views expressed in this work are solely those of the author and do not necessarily reflect the views of the publisher and the publisher hereby disclaims any responsibility for them.

Table of Contents

Nichole Jackson
Darnell (Murda) Jones
Nichole
Murda
Nichole
Murda
Nichole
Murda
Amber
Nichole
Murda
Nichole
Murda
Nichole
Amber
Anthony (Animal) Taite
Murda
Nichole
Amber
Nichole
Amber
Murda
Nichole
Murda
Amber
Murda
Nicole

Sneak Peak: A Crazy Ghetto Love Story 3

Acknowledgement

First off and foremost I have to thank God who is the head of my life and household. I will never stop because he has brought me too far! I can't and I won't go back to how things use to be. I know as long as I keep God first I am untouchable. With God with me, who can be against me?

To my children: Aaliyah, Alannah and Jaye! I love you guys with every fiber in me! Y'all are going to have some awesome childhood memories because you know your silly mommy will make everything worthwhile. Always remember us in the living room playing "Who Says" by Selena Gomez with Aaliyah on the air horn, Alannah on the air drums, mommy on the air guitar and Jaye watching and laughing. We were singing our hearts out and laughing the whole time. Don't ever forget our tickle fights or prayer time either. Remember to always keep God first and allow him to lead the way.

To my family: Geesh you guys are the freaking best! You're totally awesome! Don't ever change.. I love you!! Baby Brother Charles, I wish you were closer so I could get on your nerves daily! I love you and no amount distance can ever change that! Hopefully I'll see you soon because I'm missing you twin!

To my friends: My extra crazy friends! I remember how I met each one of you and I wouldn't change it for nothing in the world. Jasmine go ahead and have me a God child to love on because Jaye getting big now lol. Trinisha, your gonna be missing Payton because she's gonna be at my house so much!

Shameek, you have had faith in me from the very beginning! I know for a fact I won't stop because you won't let me! LOL! Any day so far that I wanted to take a break you shoot me an inspiring text that makes me say forget a break! Let me write the next chapter! And as a result another book is born!

MAJOR SHOUTOUT GOES TO: Brandon Miles and Jarelle Davis for writing all of the freestyles in my book! They didn't have to take time out of their lives to do it but they did! I'll always have y'all backs because you guys got mines! #MSGULFCOAST #228 #SUPPORT

ONLY THE HOOD WILL HELP THE HOOD!

To my readers: I'm so happy you're still riding with me! I'm trying to be your favorite author's favorite author! LOL! I hope you enjoy! I wanted to try something different. Leave a review and let me know what you think.

Random Book Fact# I changed the title 3 times before I was happy with the way it fit with the story

Nichole Jackson

Every day that I wake up in this small, cramped up 3-bedroom apartment is another day I wish I was somewhere else. It's bad enough that I'm 17 years old and have to share a room with my 19-year-old sister, Antoinette! If that isn't bad enough for you, try picturing my 5'1", 130lb body sharing a full sized bed with Antoinette's 5'5", 185lb body and see if you understand my struggle. She's always trying to squeeze her big ass in my clothes too; so whenever I finally get something new, I hide it underneath dirty clothes in my dirty clothes hamper. I keep them separated by a clean sheet though.

Antionette isn't my only sister, there's also Sabrina, standing at 5'4" and 160lbs; but she has her own room! I guess it's because she's 21 but shit, I think that should mean move the fuck out! Now my mom Stephanie, has the other room but she hardly ever uses it. She claims she don't like to take guests in her room because she sleeps there. I think she doesn't take them back there because it's nasty as fuck.

Anyway, I stood in front of my full length, dusty cracked mirror as I got dressed for school. My red cropped top shirt goes perfectly with my bright skin. It made my green eyes sparkle slightly, giving the illusion that I'm happy. The truth is, I'm very far from it. I pulled my long curly tresses into a tight high ponytail and allowed my Chinese bang to fall in my face. I turned to the side to see how my ass looked in my skinny jeans before I slipped on my red sandals. "Perfect!" I said out loud as I crept towards our room door. I had to make sure I didn't wake Nette up or I'd have to fight her before school again and I didn't feel like it.

I opened the room door and the sight before me made me vomit in my mouth. I swallowed it back down and the taste made my eyes water. I stood in the doorway of my room as I watched my mom on all fours throwing that ass in a circle on one of the local dope boys, Pee Wee's dick. They were both moaning loudly without a care in the world. I walked back into my room because I know better than to interrupt mama while she's making bill money. The last time I interrupted her I ended up going to school with her handprint on my face. I treaded slowly to my window and stared out, watching the corner boys do their thing. A slow smile began to spread across my face when Murda pulled up in his black on black Cadillac Escalade on 26" rims. He climbed out of the truck like he owned every building on the block and I began to wonder what it would be like to be his girl.

I could hear a beat in my head as I began to freestyle while watching Murda from my window:

God! Why my life like this? Who chose these hands that I fight with? Frightening days I'm tender. Lonely? My nights is! Losing my love or loving all that I lose. His swag, body, aggression, what am I supposed to do? Uh! Will he protect me, hug me tight and caress me? Or stress me, take off like my father and just neglect me? Check! I'm 17 but my problems much older. It's hard to focus with the world on my shoulder. Tired of crying, tired of living in fear. Mama fucking for crumbs like I ain't even much here. Sick of living in the hood but I ain't got a choice. I know I'm trapped inside the trap but I'mma have a voice.

I heard Nette groaning in her sleep and cut my freestyle short before she woke up completely. I rushed to the door just as Pee Wee was leaving. When I got halfway down the flight of stairs, I realized I forgot my book bag. I hauled ass back up the stairs and into our small, cramped apartment. I ran directly into my mama as she was getting her underwear out of her behind. I shook my head at the thought of her not having time to take them off, so he slid them to the side. I sucked my teeth and continued past her when I was yanked backwards by my ponytail.

"Bitch, who you suckin' yo teeth at?!" my mama gritted in my face. Spit flew from her mouth and landed on my nose but that was nothing compared to her breath. I didn't respond because I didn't want to throw up in her face. I held my breath as I waited for her to let me go. She roughly pushed my head back as tears began to build up behind my eyes. "You gone have ta start pullin' yo weight 'round here!" she yelled at my back.

I ignored her because I didn't know what she meant. I was aggravated because I was already running late and now I would have to fix my hair and run to the bus stop. I grabbed my hard hair brush off of our six drawer dresser that was missing two drawers and began fixing my ponytail. I worked real fast to get back right before I glanced in the mirror. Once I was sure I looked ok, I grabbed my purse and backpack and ran down the flight of stairs for the second time that morning.

As soon as I exited the building door, I could hear the bus coming so I hauled ass to make sure I didn't miss it. We don't have a school bus that comes to this neighborhood, it's a city bus that stops at the corner. If you're not there when the bus rolls in they just won't stop. I've seen them do a slow roll plenty of times because they're trying not to get robbed. In those times, you would be quick to get pulled off on. I use to tell Ms. Franklin all the time how strong her pull off game was until her old ass pulled off on me and I had to walk all the way to school. Now I shoot daggers at her with my eyes every time I get on the bus.

Bam! I ran full speed into something and the ground hard. It hurt so bad when I came in contact with the ground that I wanted to cry. My hands burned something serious as I looked up into the dark, cold eyes of Murda. His facial features softened as he extended his hand to help me up. I frowned at him and swatted his hand out of my face. "Move!" I said as I rolled my eyes and stormed past him. I took off in a sprint again and made it to the bus stop just in time.

It was just my luck that after running all the way to the bus stop, there would be no seats available. I stood in the aisle and held the rail as I panted heavily so I could catch my breath. As many mornings as I've had to run to the bus stop, I should be used to it, but I'm not. I looked around at the passengers briefly and noticed there were a few eyes on me. I could see clearly that three men were checking me out and I don't blame them.

See I know I'm bad, but my current home situation won't allow me to date. I can't bring anyone over to my house and I have to be home every day by 7pm. School lets out at 3:30 and by the time I make it back to my neighborhood, it's almost 5 o'clock. Then I have homework, I shower;

then go to bed so I can wake up and do it all over again.

I have two best friends that I know everything about but they don't know anything about me. Well, I guess I'm their best friend. I guess I find it extremely hard to trust people because I know the kind of things my oldest sister, Sabrina has done to people that she claims she rides for.

Anyway, my best friends are Bianca James and Amber Thompson. You ever have that best friend that you're closer too? Well that's Amber because she's so much more down to earth than Bianca is. Amber is light skinned and slightly shorter than me, standing at 5 feet even. She's chunky but very beautiful, she just doesn't know it. Bianca is dark skinned with a big butt and big breasts. She's taller than us both, standing at 5'4" with a gap toothed smile and a tongue ring. Amber is the quiet one out of the group but she has the quickest temper. It takes little to nothing to set her off and it's funny as hell to watch her scrap.

Bianca has a big mouth and her bark is way harder than her bite! She's one of those people that will scare you off during the argument but if that didn't work, she would act like she didn't have time to fight. Me, well I'm just me. I'm pretty sure there are people at school that don't like me, but no one has ever picked with me. I've never been in a fight outside of fighting my sister Antoinette, so I really don't know what I can do.

"You getting off?" Ms. Franklin asked me as she looked at me in the mirror. I nodded my head and quickly made my way to the front of the bus so

I could get off and walk the rest of the way to West High School in Memphis, Tennessee.

As I made my way up the block, I could hear loud music blaring from the speakers of a car driving up behind me. If it was anything other than Nicki Minaj, I would have ignored it but I knew it was only Amber. I quickly hopped in the back because Bianca was in the front seat.
"I don't know why you won't let me just pick you up from home girl. It will save you some time." Amber said but I didn't respond.
I just nodded my head to beat of Nicki Minaj and Ciara's song that's called "I'm Legit". We pulled in the parking lot and agreed to link up during lunch so we could chat like we did every day at school.

Darnell (Murda) Jones

I woke up early in a good ass mood this morning and I have no idea why. Shit, I really don't have shit not to be in a good mood about because all my traps jumping! I'm 26 years old with no kids, a couple of houses and a couple of bitches. I really don't have my ass on these hoes though because I'm focused on the money. Ever since I was a little gent, I wanted to be a rapper but growing up in the hood, the streets took over.

I was born into this shit, so it's most definitely true when some niggas say the streets chose them. Back in the day, my granddad ran the streets of Memphis with an iron fist until he passed away from colon cancer. He left everything to my dad, Donnie and his twin brother Ronnie. Together they groomed me to run it so they could chill out once I was ready.

See me, I don't leave nothing to chance or no stone unturned; especially when there's a snake in my midst. You know what? That may be what I'm so happy about. I finally caught up to Pee Wee's little egg muffin head ass. I recently put him over a trap house on the east side but when Animal, my right hand man, went to collect from him Wednesday, he was gone. Nothing was missing from the trap house and he wasn't short. My problem was and still is that he wasn't there. Anything could have happened and I'm normally not a could have, would have ass nigga. Right now, I'm a should have ass nigga because Pee Wee should have had his ass in that trap house with at least four soldiers backing him up.

It's now Friday and the nigga is still missing in action. I know I made a mistake and let Toto know that I was looking for him without thinking that Toto is his cousin. Yesterday, I ran up in Toto's shit and fucked him up something serious just because I thought he opened his mouth to Pee Wee. This nigga denied it the whole time I was kicking his ass in front of his baby mama and three-year-old son, so I believed him. Well I hope he wouldn't lie but aye to be real, he knows I would have murked him and his whole family on the spot had he admitted to running his mouth about some shit he ain't have nothing to do with.

Animal hit me up last night and let me know that Pee Wee be hitting this old thot broad not far from the trap house and that's why I'm up. My plan is to swing through and catch him on his way out. We're going to snatch his ass up and see what his problem is, then solve it for him.

I got in the shower and sent Animal a text to let him know I was on my way. He hit me back to let me know he was already there and confirmed that Pee Wee was inside at that very moment. See, this is why Animal is my nigga! I'll never let anyone know my every move but Animal knows enough to help me run shit. He's the only one that has met the connect outside of my bloodline and Pablo likes him too.

Animal is one of them big, muscular niggas that his presence alone puts fear in most. Shit his ass is taller than me and I'm 6'1"! A lot of people hear his name and think they call him that because he must look like some type of animal, but it's the way he kills you and leaves on the side of the road like an animal. The funny thing is, the nigga can kill you in your home and will still dump your body on the side of the road. I think he be hoping that an animal will come and eat on their corpse and in most cases they do.

I drove through the quiet streets with money on my mind. I needed to figure out if I was going to trust someone else to step up and run Pee Wee's trap house or close it down all together. I have more than enough money to close it and still be good, but a lot of my revenue comes from his house. That's probably why I'm so pissed off about him leaving it unattended. I know nothing was missing but nothing was made during his absence either and that's fucking with me.

I need to call a meeting so I can make an example out of Pee Wee, especially in front of Toto. See I'm a boss and not one that rules with fear alone, I need everyone in my organization to respect me and fear me. Not only that, but I make everybody feel like family from the runners all the way up to Animal. I don't treat anyone any different but they all know once you cross me you die. I have rules set in place for a reason and that's to keep everybody safe and hopefully out of jail. When you do shit like leave a trap house unattended, you're breaking a rule that didn't need to be told. I just don't feel like I should have to tell a nigga not to leave his post, especially if he's there alone. See Pee Wee got too comfortable so now he thinks he can get away with murder, but it's time to bring him down a few notches. I need to let them know that their lives are safe but only when they follow my rules.

Shit, I don't even let niggas leave the organization for shit. Once you're in, you're in until you die. Once you express that you want out, I'll ask if you're sure and once you say yes, you'll die. It's just that simple for me. I can't have you leaving my organization and going to one of my rivals and telling them all of my secrets. Like I said before, I don't leave anything up to chance. Shit you can retire, but only after a certain age and I have to be sure that you're going to retire. I only said that because my pops and Uncle Ronnie retired but not before they handed the reigns over to me. That means I can't retire until I've handed them same reigns over to Animal. In other words, you can't retire until there's no more room on the ladder for you to go up. Shit, even Pops and Unc still oversee shit for me from time to time.

I pulled up on the block in my all black Cadillac Escalade on 26" rims. I parked and hopped out the truck and walked around the corner where I knew Animal would be. See, he got this little bitch named Brittany that lives over here and I'm almost certain that's how he knew where to find Pee Wee. Brittany is bad as a mother fucker but she's messy as hell! It's nothing she doesn't know about anybody! I hate bitches like that. The ones that have so much to say about everybody else but ain't got shit going for themselves. She ain't got a pot to piss in or a window to throw it out of, but she can tell you how trifling or lazy everybody else is.

As soon as I rounded the corner, I saw them boys turn on the block. I dug my hands in my pocket and tossed the vials of heroin that I had in the bushes conspicuously and turned back around. I patted myself down like I forgot something in case they were watching me as I made my way back to my truck. I was walking so fast that I didn't even see the bright skinned chick until she hit the ground. I almost snapped on her for not watching where she was going until I got a good look at her. She was a true red bone, with long hair, green eyes and a perfect set of teeth. I could tell she was mixed with something but I had no idea what.

I reached my hand out to help her up but she slapped it away and I almost slapped her ass back on the ground but she stormed away too fast. I looked behind me and watched her haul ass to the city bus with a book bag on her back. "Damn, she a young buck." I said out loud to myself as I looked up at the building Animal told me Pee Wee's old freak lives in.

I headed inside the building just as the police came around the corner. I smiled to myself as I walked up the flight of stairs. I couldn't understand how anyone would live here under these conditions. Now don't get me wrong, children that live here have no choice but most of the adults in this building are living here because they're too sorry to get out and get it. If I had no choice but to live here, I'd at least clean the stairwell out. It would take nothing for them to come together as a community and keep shit clean.

When I reached the apartment door number 143, I walked straight in without knocking on the door. The living room looked a hot mess and I didn't want to walk any further into the apartment but I was on a mission to find Pee Wee. I made my way through the living room and kicked the clothes that were on the floor out of my way. I opened the door to the first bedroom on the left and saw the neighborhood hoe, Antoinette fast asleep on a bed. She's a pretty girl, so I wonder why she's out here fucking out of both ends. "At least the room's clean." I said out loud to myself as I closed the door back.

As I passed the bathroom, I could hear the shower running but I had two more rooms to check before I came back to the bathroom. The last two rooms were directly across the hall from each other and one of the doors was wide open. I walked halfway in and the stench made me back all the way back out into the hallway. I scanned the room with my eyes and knew Pee Wee wasn't in here. I can't believe he would even fuck with a bitch that's living like this. I opened the door to the last room and as soon as the chick turned around she started screaming. I stared at her naked body for a brief second as I took her in. She had a caramel complexion with bright red hair that made her otherwise organic sex appeal, pop! She had tattoos all over her body and the piercings she had that I could see were so sexy.

"Shut the fuck up!" I said as I stood in the hallway. I didn't want Pee Wee to make it out of the bathroom before I had a chance to grab him up. "What's your name?" I asked in a softer tone once I noticed her body trembling as she cupped her small breasts in her hands.

She looked at me with doe shaped eyes and fear written across her beautiful face. "Sabrina." she answered softly but I heard her nonetheless.

"Is Pee Wee here?" I asked her with a stoic expression on my face. I was seriously trying not to think about her being naked and it was proving to be harder than I thought. I allowed my mind to think about the living room and I didn't even care about her looks or the fact that she was naked because she lives here.

I glanced around her room after she shrugged her shoulders to let me know she didn't know. I closed the door back and walked swiftly to the bathroom and opened the door. The old hoe that be fucking all the dope boys was in the shower alone.

"Who in here?" she asked without sliding the dirty ass shower curtain out of the way so she could see. "Got dammit close da fuckin' door!" she snapped and I imagined she was mad because I was letting cool air in the bathroom with her.

It took her longer than expected but she finally snatched the curtain to the side with a serious mean mug on her face. Well, until she saw me standing in her doorway. A slow smile spread across her face as she took me in.

"Hey Murda! You tryna join me?" she asked as she sat one of her legs on the side of the tub exposing her wolf pussy.

My face frowned up in disgust as I walked up on her, grabbed her hair and snatched her out of the tub. A small scream escaped her lips but she quickly regrouped as her feet slipped on the tiled floor. I stopped her from falling by gripping her hair tighter, pulling her the rest of the way out of the bathroom.

I snatched her down the hall, back into the living room with her gripping my hands the whole way there. I threw her on the couch and she spread her legs for me and slid one hand between them. I watched her use her fingers to spread her pussy lips apart and almost threw up in my mouth. I cocked back and punched her old ass in the stomach.

"Where's Pee Wee?" I asked as she balled up and held on to her stomach.

She had tears streaming down her cheeks so I knew she was in a lot of pain and quite frankly, that was the goal. She shook her head and I didn't know if she was trying to say she didn't know or if she wasn't going to tell me. I cocked back and slapped her across the head.

"I don't want to hurt you Stephanie. I'm just looking for my lil homie." I said to her as I looked down at her laying in the fetal position on the couch.

"He just left." she said and I left without responding.

I know you're thinking a nigga wrong for how I just did Stephanie but shit, a nigga gotta do what he got to do. I use to have exceptions and they were women, children and old people but after Slim tortured my mama, I stopped giving a fuck. Every time I go visit her and she can't stop trembling, my heart grows colder. Every time I see her with prosthetic legs, my heart grows colder. She hasn't said a word since the shit happened to her and that makes everything worse. If I could bring Slim back to life and torture his ass all over again, I would. My only regret is not killing his entire family in front of him.

As soon as I made it out the building, my cell phone started ringing. I pulled it out of my pocket and saw that it was Animal calling.

"Yo?" I said into the receiver.

"Where you at? I got the package." he said and I smiled as I headed to my truck.

"Call a meeting." I said then disconnected the call.

I could feel someone looking at me, so I scanned the scene but didn't see anyone. I started looking at windows when my eyes landed on a window on the second floor. There stood Sabrina looking almost angelic as she stared down at me from her bedroom window.

Nichole

First and second block went by so fast at school and I was headed to the cafeteria to link up with my girls. When I walked through the double doors, I quickly scanned the room for them but didn't see either one of them. I stood in line alone, which is something I hadn't done in a while, and just watched the other students interact with each other. I'm not popular but everyone knows who I am. I just never linked up with any of them other than Bianca and Amber.

I could feel someone staring at me but as far as I could see, nobody was looking at me at all. I glanced back towards the door and saw Amber walk in and scan the room just as I had. I quickly waved her over and saw a smile spread across her face as she approached me.

"Hey boo! How was your day?" Amber asked as she gave me a hug.

This was an everyday routine for us but today it wasn't going to go as planned. I knew this because I could still feel someone staring at me.

"I'm good sweets. How are you?" I asked as I continued to look around the cafeteria.

Amber noticed what I was doing and turned around to get ready. "What's going on?" she said in an easy, low tone.

"I feel somebody staring at me." I said as I moved up with the line.

I looked back and Amber hadn't moved up with me. I watched the girl behind her sigh dramatically and roll her eyes.

"You don't want to do that!" Amber said without looking at the girl.

See Amber is pretty, short and chunky; now people have tried her before but it didn't take too long before bitches learned to respect her gangsta. If you ever wanted to know the definition of a true ride or die friend it's, Amber.

"Do you know them?" Amber asked and pointed on the far side of the cafeteria.

I looked in the direction and it took a minute before I knew who it was and rolled my eyes.

"Yea, that's Kisha. My sister Nette was messing with her sister's boyfriend, Tim." I said as I shook my head.

I was hoping Amber would let them make it but I should have known, better being as though she's a hothead.

She took off in the direction of the table that sat Kisha and three of her friends and I followed suit.

"We got a problem?" Amber asked as soon as she was within earshot.

"Oooh shit." I heard someone shout from a table near us.

I wanted to stop Amber but I didn't want anyone to think I was weak. See, I hate fighting Nette so I avoid fights every chance that I get. It's like being friends with Amber sometimes puts me in situations that I don't want to be in.

"Get out my face Pikachu!" Kisha said to Amber and everybody within earshot erupted with laughter.

"Stand up." Amber said as she took a step closer to the table.

Damien stood up on the table next to the one Kisha was sitting at and started chanting "fight" over and over in an extreme childish way. I rolled my eyes at his antics and got on guard when Kisha stood up.

I'm used to fighting Nette but I'm a little nervous about fighting someone who isn't family. Hell, Nette probably takes it easy on me because I'm family.

"You don't want it with me Pikachu! And this bitch here is a hoe just like her sister, so yeah we got a problem!" Kisha said to Amber but she was staring me down the entire time.

Fear swept through my body as the thought of this big amazon looking bitch hitting me crossed my mind. I took a deep breath and swung with all of my might.

"Get her ass Nicki!" Amber yelled.

I wasn't sure what to do next because I never remember what happens when I fight Nette, so I just kept swinging. Kisha was swinging back fast but she wasn't connecting, then I felt a hard punch in the back of my head.

"Oh hell naw! Ain't no jumping!" Amber screamed and hit the girl who had hit me.

When I turned back around to face Kisha, she hit me hard in my eye and I went into what I know now as beast mode. I don't remember anything else until I was being pulled off of a bloody, bruised and beaten Kisha who was lying across the cafeteria floor. It took a minute for me to realize that security had me suspended over his shoulder and another one had Amber. I quickly calmed down and shook my head in disappointment. *"I should have walked away."* I thought to myself as I was carried to the principal's office.

Principal Bell kept asking me what happened since I had never been in trouble before, but I wouldn't answer him. Hell I grew up in the hood and I still live there, so I know that snitching is never ok. Amber and I both got suspended for 5 days.

"What the hell am I going to tell my mama?" I asked out loud once we got in the car and the reality of being suspended for 5 days hit me.

My mama is already crazy and already made a comment that didn't sit too well with me this morning, so I really don't want to tell her.

"Girl I was just thinking the same thing!" Amber said as she looked over at me.

Now had Bianca been with us, whose mom really doesn't care what she does at all, we would have been able to sit at her house all day.

"Where the hell was Bianca?" I asked as I looked at Amber with the side eye.

"She's always conveniently not around when shit goes down, in case you haven't noticed." Amber said as she drove through traffic.

"I have an idea." Amber said before I could respond to her comment about Bianca. I watched her pull her phone out of her purse as I sat back and thought about what had just transpired. I just got in my first real fight and won! A bitch can't tell me nothing right now! On the bad side though, I got sent home early and suspended for five days.

"Hey Anthony." Amber cooed into the phone, distracting me from my thoughts. "I need a favor baby." she said and shocked me.

I knew Amber was dating someone but I had never heard her talk to him or seen him, so I kind of thought she was just making shit up.

"I need the keys to one of your clean cribs. Me and my girl got into a fight at school, got sent home early and suspended for five days, so we going to need to chill there every day during school hours." she explained as I listened to her one sided conversation.

She looked over at me while she was driving and pointed at the phone then rolled her eyes playfully. I laughed until the car swerved a little bit, then my face filled with alarm. She laughed at me as she focused on the road. "Nothing baby, I was laughing at my scary ass friend." she said to him. "Yeah I can come get it right now. Where 'bout?" she asked and made a face at that I didn't understand it. "Ok, we're on our way." she said as she turned off on an exit and drove in the opposite direction. She played Nicki Minaj all the way to this big ass warehouse.

My mouth hit the floor when I saw all of the expensive cars parked outside of the warehouse. We parked next to a red, candy paint Ferrari and I felt broker than I am. She climbed out of the car and looked at me like something was wrong with me. "What?" I asked with a stank look on my face.
"First of all, Kisha rocked yo ass bitch, so don't make faces right now." she said and we cracked up with laughter.
"Fuck you!" I said back to her in between laughs. "Second of all, come on so you can meet my Ant baby!" she said then started twerking for no reason at all. I got so tickled because sometimes she just does that. I just chalk it up to excitement.

I climbed out of the car slowly and tried to steal a sneak peek at my eye but Amber caught me and started laughing again. "Bitch fuck you!" I said

as I folded my arms across my chest. I was pouting so hard until she threw her arms around me and started smiling really bright in my face until I started laughing with her. "Is it that bad?" I asked right before she opened the warehouse door.
"Yes now c'mon." she said then lead the way inside of the warehouse.

I could hear chatter from a room that was off to the side. Amber opened the door and I followed her in. It looked like a meeting had either taken place or was about to take place. I noticed this brown skinned dude whose hair looked like he was starting his dreads off, sitting in the corner with this faraway look in his eyes. I only noticed him because he was the only person that wasn't chatting with anyone else.

I focused my attention back on Amber as I watched her walk up to this huge, monstrous looking guy that was sitting with his back to us on the table, chopping it up with someone else. She wrapped her arms around him, then he turned around and gave her smile. I didn't expect him to be as handsome as he is from how big he was from behind. He stood to his feet and had to bend all the way over just to allow her to wrap her arms around his neck.

I smiled at how happy she is at this very moment and crossed my fingers that one day I'd be able to love freely.
"C'mere Nichole." she said to me then looked between Anthony and I. I approached them slowly and she introduced us. I shook his hand and asked if I could use the bathroom because I had to go super bad. He gave me directions but I forgot on my way out because I locked eyes with the guy that was looking spaced out when we first walked in. I

walked down the hall and opened each door and took a peek in. When I opened the third door, shock filled my body and I couldn't move even if I wanted to.

"I'm sorry man! Please man! I'll never leave the trap house like that again! Just give me one more chance!" Pee Wee pleaded to some tall guy.

I stared on, my mind was telling me to walk away but my feet weren't listening. Pee Wee was beat up pretty bad, but being as though I see him most of my mornings fucking my mama, I can recognize him.

"I'm not Biggie my nigga. He may give you one more chance." he said in a sing song voice like he was singing that old "One more chance" song. I watched in horror as he raised his gun.

"Help me!" Pee Wee said as he looked directly at me.

A bullet to his head killed him instantly. His body slumped over in the chair that he was tied down too.

The guy turned around and looked at me with cold dark eyes. "Murda." I said out loud as tears welled up in my eyes. My flight or fight senses kicked in as I slammed the door shut and took off inside the next room. I locked the door and ran into one of the bathroom stalls. I know this is not the time to piss but if I didn't go I was going to piss on my damn self.

Murda

I'm hardly ever the one to call the meetings but I'm always the person that leads them. After I told Animal to call a meeting, he did and told me he would meet me there with the package. See when we have on call meetings, Animal only calls the people that are over a trap house or territory. Today we are having one of those on calls meetings. Now on the 6th of each month, we have a regular meeting in which everyone is expected to be there. You can only miss three meetings before you're cut out of my organization. I hope you remember what happens to those who leave the organization.

Anyway, I pulled up to the warehouse at the same time as Animal. I watched him climb out of his car and pop the trunk. I smiled the biggest smile that I had smiled that day as I approached the trunk. I peered inside of it and saw Pee Wee lying unconscious with tape covering his mouth. I scooped his body up out of the trunk and threw him over my shoulder. Animal came around and closed the trunk, then lead the way to the warehouse. I waited patiently as he unlocked the doors and moved out of my way.

"I'm fina set shit up in here. They'll be here in a minute." Animal said to me.

I nodded my head and headed towards what we call the interrogation room. When I walked in, everything I needed was already in there. I sat his body down in a chair and taped him to it. I also tied him down with rope just to be sure he wouldn't be able to break free. I slapped him around a bit to wake him up. When that didn't work, I gave him a few gut punches. His bitch ass woke up then.

"Where were you Wednesday?" I asked as I stood in front of him with my hands interlaced behind my back.

"Huh?" he asked as he looked at me sideways. "Wrong answer." I said as I punched him in the stomach again.

He gagged and coughed but nothing came up. He started to breathe extremely heavy so I waited for him to regain control.

"Where were you Wednesday?" I asked again.

"At the trap." he said as he looked directly into my eyes.

"Lie again." I said and punched him in his face.

He allowed his head to dangle in the direction that I punched him in. I hit him again to bring his face back in my direction. He groaned out in pain as he looked at me with blood dripping out of his mouth.

"Where were you Wednesday?" I asked again. I rocked from the heels of my feet to my toes, a clear sign that I was aggravated.

"At this bitch house." he said as he shook his head and started crying.

I couldn't believe this nigga was crying like a little bitch. Hell, I couldn't believe I let a bitch nigga into my organization.

Whap! I backhanded him so hard the chair fell over. I kicked him in his stomach and spit on him. "Stop crying like a bitch!" I snapped then sat the chair back up. "What bitch were you with?" I asked and he shook his head at me. I nodded my head because at least his ass is loyal to some damn body. It's funny that I already know what bitch he was with though.

"I'm going to kill you Pee Wee and it's a sad situation because you a cool as lil dude." I said to him as I shook my head at him.
"Man I'm sorry man! I won't leave the trap house unattended no more man just don't kill me!" he cried out as snot ran from his nose.

The sight before me pissed me off so bad that I just started hitting him over and over again. It took me a minute to stop but once I did, Pee Wee was barely recognizable. When he looked up at me his ass started begging all over again. He even went so far as to ask for one more chance! His ass reminded me of Faith Evans asking Biggie for one more chance. I'm not that nigga though. Then I noticed him look past me. I already felt a presence behind me, but I didn't want to let on that I knew they were there. I pulled out my .45 and shot Pee Wee. I watched his body slump over then I turned around slowly to see who was at the door.

She was so beautiful that I was momentarily caught off guard. She looked so familiar but I couldn't place her at the moment. I shrugged because I know I'll see her again. She thinks she got away but I always find who I'm looking for. *"Those eyes though."* I thought to myself as I grabbed my machete off of the shelf.

I pushed Pee Wee's head back against the chair and swung the machete. It cut him right above his clavicle. I smiled as blood and his esophagus fell out of the opening. I grabbed a black bag to slide the head inside of and carried it all to the bathroom with me.

As I was washing my hands, I thought I heard someone gasp behind me. I turned around and looked under all five stall doors but didn't see any feet. I pulled my burner back out and cocked it.

"If someone's in here and don't want to die, come out now." I said as I waited for any sign of movement.

I kicked the first door in and took aim, nothing. I kicked the second door in and took aim. I repeated the motion all the way to the fourth door but I didn't see anyone. I looked through the cracks of the last one because that's where they have to be. I kicked it in and started shooting, nothing.

"Damn I must be tripping." I said out loud as I backed away from the stall. A few seconds later, Animal came running in the bathroom followed by Boogie and Skip.

"What's popping?" Animal asked.

"Nothing man I was tripping." I said as I shook my head and followed them out of the bathroom.

Nichole

I breathed a sigh of relief once the gunfire ceased. My arms and legs were beyond tired as I balanced myself at the top of the stall right above the door. I almost shitted bricks when Murda came in the bathroom, because I thought he was looking for me. I gave myself away when I saw him because I gasped. I tried to cover my mouth but it was too late.

I jumped down and sat on the toilet so I could rub my arms and legs because they were beyond tired. I walked cautiously out of the bathroom and headed straight for the door.
"Damn bitch you had to shit?" Amber asked from behind me and started to laugh.
"Just open the door." I said as I ran quickly to my side. She hit the button to unlock the car doors and I hopped in.
"Bitch you look like you seen a ghost." Amber said as she cranked the car up. Nicki Minaj's song Bass purred through the speakers as she pulled off.

We rode in silence until Amber's phone started to ring. I watched her connect it to the Bluetooth of the car before she answered the call.
"Yeah?" she answered in an annoyed voice.
"Bitch I heard yall mufuckin' asses got in a fight hoe!" Bianca's loud, ghetto and obnoxious ass said. I shook my head and looked over at Amber.
"Yea." Amber replied in a nonchalant tone.
"So how you get Nichole's scary ass to bang witcha bitch?" Bianca asked and my jaw hit the floor.

I had no idea that she felt that way about me. I looked over at Amber and she signaled for me to be quiet.

"Bitch Nichole got them hands. If she ain't fight nobody for your scary ass, then that's just because she ain't want to." Amber said in defense to what she said about me.

"What the fuck ever! She thinks she's better than everybody. I know she be talking about me behind my back. Wait 'til I find out fasho though." Bianca said angrily into the phone.

I was literally sitting there in awe because I had no idea that she felt this way about me. I didn't know how to address it or anything.

"Bitch get off my line. Nichole is not like that and you know it!" Amber said.

"Well why we never been to her house? She probably lives in a mansion or some shit with a butler and just doesn't want us to sip champagne with her." Bianca snapped.

I shook my head because she couldn't have been further away from the truth.

"Bitch if she lived in a mansion she wouldn't ride the city bus to school dummy!" Amber snapped back and rolled her eyes.

"Bitch Nunu did it! You just up her ass!" Bianca said.

I gave Amber a confused look and realized she was confused too.

"Who is Nunu?" Amber asked.

"Bitch don't act like you ain't seen ATL!" Bianca said and Amber started laughing.

"Bitch you mad and comparing Nichole to a movie character. Ok I'm done bye." Amber said and hung the phone up.

She continued to laugh but I didn't say a word. I was pissed and confused. I thought Bianca was my friend but she really was just on the inside hating. If she knew that her home life was far better than mine, she would realize she ain't have shit to be mad at me for. I don't have company because I live in a cramped up apartment that barely has enough room in it for the people that live there. Not to mention, I never know what I will walk in on. I wouldn't be able to show my face again if my mama was caught fucking a dope boy.

"You want me to take you home?" Amber asked. I looked at her and could tell she just wanted to know where I live.
"Don't tell B where I live." I said to her and waited for her to agree.
Once she nodded her head, I gave her directions.
It was just my luck that my mama was outside talking to Ms. Brenda when we pulled up. I sighed heavily as Amber pulled over and parked her car.
"What's wrong?" Amber asked with a worried expression on her face.
"That's my mama and she gonna trip on me." I said and climbed out of the car.
I opened the back door and grabbed my backpack out of it, when I was yanked by my ponytail. I lost my balance and fell to the ground. I felt kicks all over my body.
I looked up and my mama and Ms. Brenda were both kicking me.
"So you like fighting lil bitch?" my mama yelled as she continued to kick me.

Now I know I didn't have to hide shit because either the school called or the streets talked.

"Mama stop." I said as I grabbed her leg.

Ms. Brenda kicked me so hard in the back that I lost my breath.

"What the fuck?" my mama said as she stopped kicking me.

I looked up and saw Amber was beating the shit out of Ms. Brenda.

"You like jumping people old trick?!" Amber screamed as she continued to beat the brakes off of Ms. Brenda.

I smiled inwardly because I bet she'll think twice about getting in other people's business.

"Nichole get your friend and go in the house." my mom said to me in a motherly tone.

I stood up slowly with a confused look on my face as I looked at my mother.

I limped slowly towards Amber and pulled her off Ms. Brenda. My mom rushed to Ms. Brenda's aid and helped her inside the apartment building.

"No wonder you don't have company girl!" Amber said as she caught her breath.

I was beyond embarrassed so I didn't respond right away.

"Girl it's ok. We all got shit to deal with at home. You good though?" she asked and I nodded my head. "Call me if you need anything. You know my number?" she asked and I nodded my head. I was still too embarrassed to speak. "Alright. I'm coming to get you in the morning. Ion wanna beat yo mama ass, so sneak out if you need to." Amber said then hopped in her car and sped away.

I looked up at my room window and saw Nette looking down and knew I was up for another fight once I got up the stairs. I shook my head and decided to go ahead and face it now rather than waiting until later.

As soon as I opened the door to the apartment, I was met with a swift kick to the stomach. I flew back into the hallway but was dragged back into the apartment by my mom and Nette. I started to scream at the top of my lungs because I didn't know how to fight Nette back without hitting our mom.

I began to cry as I willed myself not to fight. I balled up in a fetal position as they continued to rain blows all over my body. *"What a day."* was all I could think as I felt myself losing consciousness.

Murda

I wasn't worried about ole girl getting away from me because Memphis ain't as big as people think it is…. especially not for a nigga like me. It will take no time to find ole girl and silence her. Now that shit with the bathroom had me bugging for real though. When I first heard a noise, I thought it was ole girl but I was sure she would have come out before I started shooting. Hell I thought I killed two birds with one stone when I kicked that last stall in and started blasting.

I shook my head at the thought of how I must have looked to the people that are under my reign as I stood in front of them.

"Animal called this meeting today because niggas are getting comfortable and acting recklessly." I said in a voice that commanded attention.

All chatter ceased as soon as I started talking and that wasn't out of fear. It was out of respect.

"When we act recklessly, it puts the entire organization in jeopardy." I continued then paused as I looked around the room.

Every man made eye contact with me except for Toto. Lack of eye contact is a sign of a guilty man. "We can't have a solid building without strong foundation. It appears that we also have a leaky roof." I said as I stared at Toto.

I noticed everyone turned their attention to Toto since I was looking at him. He glanced around the room and started fidgeting with his finger…. Another sign of a guilty man. I have no idea what he told, but I know he told something and for that he must pay.

"We have rules set in place for safety. Where there isn't a rule, we must rely on common sense or face deadly consequences."

I stated as I observed the sweat form on Toto's forehead. I turned my attention away from him and began addressing everyone as a whole.

"Pee Wee left his trap house unattended." I said then paused as I waited for a reaction. My men shook their heads at the revelation. I looked at Toto and he stared down at the floor.

"Anything could have happened. We could have lost everything inside of his trap house. Luckily, nothing was stolen. Sadly, nothing was made in the amount of time that Pee Wee was gone. With that being said, that position is now up for grabs. Please submit any recommendations for who should run that house by close of business next Friday." I said then sat the bag on the table in front of me.

Everyone nodded their heads until they saw the bag. I watched confusion wash over all of their faces as I looked around the room. "Heads up Toto." I said as I tossed the bag to him. The bag slid off of Pee Wee's head in midair. I watched as his head landed directly in Toto's lap.

It took a minute, but when realization of what he was holding set in, he tossed the head on the floor and jumped out of his chair. His movement caused the chair to tip over and I think the noise of the chair hitting floor scared him because he damn near jumped out of his sneakers. I watched him intently as he looked around the room nervously. My eyes scanned the room until they connected with Skip. I waved him over and waited until he got within earshot.

"Follow him." I said and Skip walked away.

See with Skip, he never asks questions. He figures everything out that he needs to figure out through observation. You have to beware of a nigga like that if they aren't loyal. Skip is a smart ass street nigga but he's loyal to a fault! You only have to beware of people like him because you never know what's on their minds. A person that has questions that aren't voiced answers them mentally. The problem with that is, you don't know what question he has about you or how your actions answer it.

Toto ran out of the room but he didn't head for the door. I watched Skip follow him out and nodded my approval. "Ok meeting adjourned." I said then headed towards Animal. I hadn't forgotten about ole girl, I just had more pressing matters to tend to.
"Animal lemme holla at you." I said to him in a friendly tone.
"What's up?" he asked as he stood in front of me.
"You had a broad here right?" I asked just to be sure. I know it was nobody else because everybody else knows better.
"Yea. Why?" he asked as he stared into my eyes.
It wasn't on no gay shit. Real niggas know respect comes from a variety of things and a man that makes eye contact is normally an honest man.
"She had a friend with her?"
I asked and watched a smile spread across his face as he nodded his head.
"You want her?" he asked and I could already tell where he was going with this.
"Naw she saw me kill Pee Wee." I said and watched his smile vanish. It was replaced with a cold stare. I

literally watched the life drain from his eyes as I stared at him.

"Want me to handle that?" he asked as he slipped his phone out of his pocket.

"Naw I got it." I said for some strange reason. Normally I'd waste no time getting rid of problems because I didn't like to leave stuff to chance but it was something about her that piqued my interest.

"Iight bet." Animal said as he walked away.

I watched him place his phone to his ear as he sat down in the chair next to where I stood. "The hell you doing?!" he shouted into the phone as he jumped back out of the chair he had just sat in. "Who the fuck was you fighting man? You just left!" he snapped at the chick. "Oh word? Damn that's fucked up!" he said. "Yea me and my boy wanna holla at you on some real shit. Go on to the crib." he said then disconnected the call. "C'mon bruh, you drive." Animal said as he turned around to face me.

Once everyone saw us leaving, they headed out the door as well. Animal ran in and did a quick walk through to make sure nobody was left inside before we locked up. We always checked because if you're in there when we lock up, you're stuck until we come back because you can't get out. Not to mention there isn't any food.

"What happened?" I asked Animal as I hopped in the passenger seat of my truck.

I laughed at the look he gave me but I didn't know where we were going so there wasn't any point of me driving there.

"I called my bitch and she answered the phone outta breath! Say the girl she brought to the warehouse

with her mama and some lady jumped her when she took her home." Animal said to me and I shook my head.
Hell truth be told, she looked like she had already been into a fight when I saw her. She was still beautiful though.
"That's fucked up man." I said to Animal and he nodded his head in agreement.

He turned the radio up and drove all the way to one of his extra cribs on the lower east side. It's in a fairly decent neighborhood so he lets his girl crash there whenever she needs to get away from home. I personally don't know why he's so comfortable putting the dick to her little ass. I know these hot ass little girls want it, but if you can go to jail for giving it to them then stay from between them legs. At least until she's 18. I don't know if this chick is 18 yet, but I know she's still in high school.

We pulled up to the small two bedroom, flat bed house and parked next to his girl's car. I hopped out and followed him to the door.
"Hold on real quick." he said as he opened the door and peeked his head in. "Go put some clothes on I got my mans with me." he said to her.
He waited a few minutes then he opened the door all the way and walked inside.
"Oh you like this one." I said with a chuckle.
I knew he liked her because I've seen all of his bitches naked and he never cared enough to tell them to put on any clothes before. He shook his head at me and walked into the living room.
I sat on the loveseat that's against the wall that allows me to see the door and the hallway. I can't

stand for someone to walk up behind me, so I sit with my back near the wall at all times. Hell, I just got comfortable enough to get a vehicle with a backseat! A nigga ain't scared, I'm just safe.

A few minutes later, she came walking back into the living room. She waved at me then flopped down next to Animal.

"Hey Ant baby!" she said as she kissed him on the cheek.

I watched him smile at her then his facial expression went blank. I glanced over at her and her facial expression went from loving to rage. *"Yea my boy met his match."* I thought to myself.

"The fuck you looking at me like that for?!" she said as she stood to her feet.

She squared up like she was ready to go toe to toe with his ass and I just shook my head. She a little on the plump side but she's beautiful nonetheless.

"Man sit cho ass down!" he snarled at her. She rolled her eyes and placed her hand on her hip. Animal glanced over at me and I shrugged my shoulders. Shit it ain't my place to put her in check. He gotta do that on his own. I'm here about one thing and one thing only.

"My boy needa holla at you." Animal said to her. She rotated her body towards me and still maintained her dumb ass attitude. We stared at each for several seconds.

"You gone talk?" she asked.

I gave her the look I give everyone right before I kill them and Animal jumped up in her face. I watched the attitude fade away as it was replaced with fear and she continued to look at me.

"Sit down ma." Animal said to her but she was stuck in a trance.

I softened my stare and she sat on the other side of Animal. I just hope she knows that if I wanted to kill her Animal wouldn't be able to stop me.

"I'm sorry what's up?" she asked in a low tone.

I think her passive tone shocked Animal the way he looked at her. I laughed a low, deep laugh. You know the kind that starts in your gut and works its way up. Only I didn't allow it to work its way up, if that makes sense.

"You brought a chick with you to the warehouse. Who is she?" I asked her.

I watched her body tense up as I observed her movements. She sat stone faced as she stared at me without answering my question. "Who is she?" I asked again as I looked at her crazy.

"Listen, I would tell you if I thought you were interested in dating her but you're not. So, um well uh... yea." She said as she matched my stare.

I could tell she was a bit nervous but she was damn near risking her own life to save her friend's life.

"How you know I'm not interested?" I asked as I looked at her through squinted eyes.

"Because when you mentioned her, your finger twitched slightly." she answered as she nodded her head towards my right hand.

I glanced over at Animal and he looked as shocked as I was on the inside though my face remained stoic.

"She saw something she shouldn't have seen. I need her." I said as I rested my hands on my knees.

"Who seen what?" she asked with a confused look on her face.

Animal sighed dramatically as he looked between the two of us.

"Your friend." I said as I tried to keep my tone even.

I was trying to put fear in her so she would let me know who the chick was. I could see the fear, hell I could even sense it but as I watched her stare me down, I realized she has way more heart than she does fear. Her loyalty to her friend was not going to let her tell me anything against her.

"I don't do friends." she said as she stood to her feet. "Now y'all can go or I will." she said as she crossed her arms across her chest.

The only reason she's breathing right now is because of Animal. I glanced at him and could see he didn't want me to kill her but he wasn't sure of my plans.

"I'm not gone hurt her. You got my word." I said sincerely.

All a man got is his word and his balls so I always stand true to my word.

"Hurt who?" she asked with a smirk on her face.

I looked over at Animal in disbelief. I began to wonder who she's been playing hard ball with.

"You got you one bruh." I said as I walked up to Animal and gave him dap.

He stood to his feet and kissed ole girl as we walked out of the door.

I unlocked my truck door and climbed in the driver's seat and waited for Animal to get in. I pulled off, circled the block and parked down the street.

"What you doing?" Animal asked with a confused look on his face.

"She's going to go to her eventually. Until then, we're following her." I answered without taking my eyes off the door.

She stayed inside a few hours and when she came out the door, she was dressed like she was going to school. She had her book bag on and everything.

We followed her to another house and I glanced over at Animal. He didn't say a word as he watched his girl park her car and walk up to the house like she owns the place. I watched closely as she dug through her purse then threw her head back like she was aggravated. I took another glance at Animal and he looked like we weren't watching the same thing. I focused my attention back on ole girl just as the door swung open. I stared on in disbelief as a man stepped to the side to allow her enough room to enter. He stuck his head out the door then closed it.

I stole another glance at Animal and he was completely unbothered.

"Fuck this." I said out loud as I reached under my seat and grabbed my banger. I cocked it and opened the door but Animal stopped me.

"That's her dad man." Animal said as he shook his head and laughed.

I joined in on the laughter as I shut the car door back and put the gun back.

"Man I thought you were turning into a bitch on me." I said in between laughs.

"Never that! I was seeing what you were gone do." he said to me.

"What's her name?" I asked Animal.

I know if his girl brought her friend then they were introduced. I also know that Animal never forgets a name. We're polar opposites when it comes down to that. I can't ever remember names but I know when I've seen someone before. Animal on the other hand, remembers names and links them with situations. Well, unless he's known you a few years.

"Amber." he answered as he looked up at the window.

"What's her friend name?" I asked.

"Nichole." he answered without looking away from the window.

I glanced up at it and looked away once I saw she was getting undressed. I didn't want to disrespect my boy by looking at his girl. I don't like my women that big anyway but to each his own right.

"She ain't gone leave til it's time for school, so we ain't gotta stay here." Animal said to me once he tore his eyes away from the window.

I nodded my head and pulled off. "We gotta go check on the traps." I said and Animal nodded his head.

Nichole

I woke up in the living room on the floor. I shook my head when I realized they beat me until I passed out and left me there. I fought through the pain and pushed myself to a sitting position. My whole body ached, especially my head and back. I knew my eyes were swollen because I could hardly see out of either one of them.

I looked around the filthy living room as I stood slowly. The room started to spin so I took a seat on the couch. My stomach rumbled but I know there's no food here, so it may be a while before I can eat something. Normally, the only time I get to eat is when I'm at school and I go through the lunch line twice so I can eat after school.

My mama gets food stamps but she sells them to feed her habits. Maybe now that Pee Wee is gone, she will actually go grocery shopping. "Yea right." I said out loud to myself as I tried to stand again.

I made it to my room on wobbly legs. When I opened the door, I noticed Nette was asleep and it was still dark outside. I quickly grabbed some sleeping clothes, my small hand held radio and headed to the bathroom. Once I made it to the bathroom, I sighed a loud sigh of relief. The way my body felt at that moment, I knew I needed to soak in the tub and this late, I would be able to soak in peace. I turned on nothing but hot water, stripped down naked and looked in the mirror. I had to do a double take to make sure it was really me.

Tears seeped out of my swollen eyes and slid down my bruised cheeks. It burned slightly as a tear crossed the split of my busted lip. I looked gruesome and I knew I would look worse before I looked any better. I tried to look up but my eyelids wouldn't open.

I slid my body slowly into the hot water. I could feel sweat forming right above my top lip as I lay down in the water. I let the heat from the water hold me as I closed my eyes. I relinquished my mind of thoughts of everything bad and tried desperately to focus on the good.

As hard as I tried to focus on something positive in my life, there wasn't a single thing about my life that popped into my head. Hell, the only positive person I have is Amber but we only talk at school because I don't have a cell phone.

I reached up and tried to turn my radio on but sighed in disappointment when I realized the batteries were dead. I stayed in the tub until the water turned from hot to warm. I emerged my entire body underwater as I wondered what it would be like to no longer be here. I imagined being in a peaceful setting, maybe a beach, maybe as naked as I am right now sipping mimosas.

BANG! BANG! BANG! I jumped up and started coughing uncontrollably because I inhaled water on my way up. Fear gripped my body as I sat in the tub trembling and choking as I tried hard to catch my breath. "OPEN THIS DAMN DOOR!" my mom screamed as she continued to bang on the door. I calmed down quickly once I realized it was her and not someone trying to kill me. My thoughts quickly went to my near experience with Murda in the bathroom. BANG! BANG! BANG! My mom started beating on the door again. *"There goes my peaceful setting."* I said to myself as I pulled the plug to drain the water out of the tub. I quickly bathed before the water let out and hopped out of the tub. I dried my body off slowly and applied the lotion even slower. My body was still extremely sore and I didn't want to move too fast. I ignored everything my mom was saying as she yelled while I got dressed.

I swung the door open and tried to step out but she wouldn't move out of the way.
"Excuse me ma." I said with my head down as I waited for her to move.
I shook my head when I saw another pair of feet walk up. I knew it was Nette before I ever looked up into her eyes.
"Why you up running my damn water bill up?!" My mom snapped at me.
"Ma I drew a bath. I didn't take a shower." I responded in a confused tone. I don't know how in the hell me taking a bath was running her water bill up.
"You talking back bitch?!" my mom asked with an angry expression on her face.
Before I could respond, she had her hands gripped tightly around my neck as she forced her way inside of the bathroom. I gripped my hands around her wrists and tried to pry her hands from my neck but she only squeezed tighter. I glanced over at Nette when I heard laughter and couldn't believe these people are my blood relatives.

Tears stung my cheeks as my mom threw me against the wall. I wanted to fight her back but I couldn't bring myself to fight my mom. It's like an unspoken rule that's definitely forbidden.

"Fucking crybaby!" Nette screamed as she punched me in my stomach.

My mom let me go and pushed me over into the tub. I balled my body up and cried as they rained blow after blow all over the side of my body. I used my arms to shield my head but that left my side wide open and they took advantage of that.

"What the fuck!" I heard Sabrina yell. "STOP!" she screamed at the top of her lungs then the beating stopped.

"You always up her ass!" Nette said.

I wanted to turn around and look but I didn't want them to start beating me again.

"Get the fuck out!" Sabrina snapped. A few seconds later I heard the bathroom door slam shut.

"Ouch!" I cried out as Sabrina helped me out of the tub.

I kept my head down as she sat me down on the toilet. She squatted down in front of me and looked up into my face. I stared at her with tears streaming down her face as she examined mines.

"I'm sorry Nichole." she said as she shook her head. "I don't know why they hate you but you can't stay here." she whispered softly in my ear.

"Where will I go?" I asked her. She looked away which let me know that she had no idea.

"One day they won't stop Nichole. One day they will kill you." she said as she placed her arms around me softly.

  I cried harder at the realization of the choice set before me. I was in a lose-lose situation. If I stayed, eventually they would kill me but if I left, the streets would. "C'mon." Sabrina said as she pulled me up to my feet.

She leads the way into her room and allowed me to sit on her bed. "Do you have clothes?" she asked and I nodded my head. I told her where she could find them and she left out of her room to go get them. I could hear her and Nette going back and forth over my things but I dared not move. Sabrina returned and stuffed all of my things in a garbage bag and gave me a pair of shoes. "Do what you got to do to survive." she said as she stuffed money down in my panties. "You gotta go now." she said and I just nodded my head.

I stood to my feet and pulled her into a tight embrace.
"Thank you." I said as I pulled away.
She handed me a shoebox, "Don't open this until you're somewhere safe." she said as she shoved it in my arms. I was a bit skeptical about the box but I took it anyway.

Sabrina helped me out of the door and down the steps. "Good luck. I love you." Sabrina said to me. I didn't respond because I doubt very seriously that anyone could ever love me.

I grabbed the bag with what little strength I had left and walked up to the corner. "I guess I'll just sit here at the bus stop until the next bus runs." I said quietly to myself. I'm normally asleep around this time so I have no idea when the next one would run. I sat my bag of clothes on the ground in front of the bench and laid across it with my box gripped tightly in my arms.

__Murda__

      Animal and I rode around to all my traps and did pop ups to make sure everybody was on point. Luckily for them, they were. I cruised through the streets of Memphis with no real destination in mind. I ended up back at the warehouse so I let Animal get out to get in his own whip.
"Aye." Animal called out before I had a chance to pull off.
"Yea?" I answered as I rolled the window down.
"You gone kill her?" he asked as he looked directly in my eyes. I could tell he either really likes Amber or he loves her.
"I said I wouldn't hurt her." I answered.
"Yea but are you gone kill her? Nigga I know you." he said as he stared at me.
I couldn't help but laugh at him because he knows I consider quick kills painless. So if I say I won't hurt someone, it doesn't mean that they will still live.
"I don't know yet." I answered honestly.
He nodded his head and walked over to his car. I checked the time and it nearing 3a.m. I pulled off so I could go home and get at least three hours of sleep so I could make it back to Amber's parent's house.

      As soon as I turned on my street, my cell phone started ringing.
"Yeah?" I answered without looking at the screen to see who it was.
"Aye my nigga we got a sexy lil piece here for ya." the caller said. I pulled the phone away from ear and saw that it was the little nigga Razor.

"Oh yeah?" I asked with sarcasm evident in my voice because I really didn't give a fuck.

"Yeah man, we over at the eastside trap." he said. I didn't respond because I thought I heard screaming in the background.

"Aye don't touch her yet. Let Boss hit it first." Razor said to someone.

"Yo who there with you?" I asked as I turned the truck around.

"Juice, Rocket and Tuff." he said then I heard him smack his lips like a bitch. "Man chill the fuck out man don't touch her! Boss on his way!" he checked someone.

"I'll be there in fifteen minutes. Don't nobody touch her." I said then hung the phone up before he had a chance to respond.

I drove like a bat out of hell all the way to the trap house. When I pulled up, I looked up at the window of the apartment that the old thot lives in. I scanned the other windows and when I didn't see anyone, I walked on down to the trap house. I never park directly in front of any one of my trap houses, it's a precaution.

Before I had a chance to knock, Razor swung the door open. Every time I see this little nigga I wonder who cut his face like that and why. As my thoughts drifted to the girl they done snatched and were about to rape, I think I have a good guess as to why it happened.

I dapped him up and made my way inside of the house. When I walked in the living room, I took mental notes of the looks they gave me even though they all spoke. I gave them each a head nod and turned my attention to Razor.

"Where she at?" I asked and watched his slow smile spread into a big cheesy grin.

This nigga was excited about raping someone and I just didn't understand why. It's plenty of bitches that's fucking willingly, so why take it from someone who doesn't want to give it up? I'll never understand the mind frame of a rapist.

I followed Razor into the room, the sight before me made my blood boil instantly. Her body was banging, no doubt, but they didn't have to beat her like this. I couldn't tell if I knew the woman or not but I knew one thing for sure and two things for certain. I was not about to rape this woman or any other woman for that matter and neither were they.

"Why yall beat her like that?" I asked with a frown on my face.

"Man with all due respect, fuck all that. Go on, beat that pussy up so we can go next." he said as he bounced his head slightly as he talked.

As I stared at him and watched his movements for a few seconds, I realized he was high as the mile-high club at this very moment.

"Did you pay for it?" I asked as I looked at him. He frowned his head in confusion as he looked at me. "Whatever the fuck you on right now. Nigga did you pay for it?" I reiterated. I stood there and watched the color drain from his face but I decided to keep my cool, for now. "Y'all load her up for me and come take a ride with me." I said with a smile.

Everybody seemed eager to ride but Juice. I could tell he was unsure of what was about to happen and didn't want to go.

"Aye Juice man you sure you don't want to hit?" Razor asked.

I stared at Juice intently because his answer would decide his fate.

"Naw man I got a daughter. No disrespect to you-" Juice paused as he looked at me, "But this shit is sick yo! I'm good." he said with a deep from etched in his face. I nodded my head and waited for them to load her up.

"Nigga she ain't yo daughter though!" Razor pressed the issue.

"She ain't gotta be nigga. You simple minded bruh! I tried putting y'all ruthless ass niggas on game when y'all brought her in here." he snapped as he stood there mugging the fuck out of Razor.

Rocket and Tuff walked out holding her unconscious body in their arms. I shook my head at the fact that he took both of them to lift her up.

"Let me grab her shit." Razor said as he walked to the back of the house.

"What you just put in there?" I asked with a confused expression on my face.

"She had a garbage bag and a shoe box. I wanted to make sure she had all of her things when we got done." Razor said and it shocked the fuck out of me. I nodded my head even though I didn't understand the logic of kidnapping and raping a person but making sure their things were together for them. When I glanced over at Juice, he also had a look of confusion on his face.

"Alright let's go." I said as I headed out the door. Razor was behind me but Juice was just standing there. "Juice man, c'mon." I said to him in a cold tone.

"I got a daughter man." he said as he tried to explain why he didn't want to come.

"I didn't ask you shit about your personal life." I said then walked off. I didn't have to turn around to know if he followed suit because he huffed and puffed all the way to the truck. "It's unlocked." I said to the dummies that stood next to the truck holding a body.

I glanced up at the windows and saw the neighborhood hoe was watching. When she saw me look up at her, she quickly closed the curtains. I shook my head and hopped in the truck.

"Juice, get up front." I said to him just as Razor opened the front door.

I watched Razor roll his eyes and hop in the back with Tuff. I noticed Rocket was all the way in the back with the girl. "Don't touch her nigga!" I said as I looked at him through my rear view mirror. He frowned his face up at me but he held his hands up in a "I surrender" type of fashion.

I pulled my phone out of my pocket and sent a text message then pulled off. I rode blasting that mixtape called Islah that Kevin Gates just put out. Any time I'm about to kill a few mu'fuckers, I use music to ease my mind. I've always had a love for music but life has gotten in the way. One day I'm going to figure out exactly what I want to do in the music industry though.

"Is that Animal?" Razor asked as we pulled into the warehouse's parking lot.

"Yea." I answered as I stepped out of the truck.

"Damn I wanted to get seconds." Razor said as he

shook his head in disappointment. I ignored his ass and headed over to a pissed off Animal.

"Play it cool bruh. Juice lives." I whispered in Animal's ear as I gave him dap. He looked over my shoulder and nodded his head then walked towards the warehouse doors to unlock it. "Bring her in." I said as I followed Animal inside.

"Man what's going on?" Animal asked with a frown on his face.

"Man we gotta kill all these niggas except Juice." I said as I checked behind me to make sure they weren't there.

"Why?" Animal asked with a confused look on his face.

"You'll see. Just play by ear." I answered just as Razor walked through the door with a smile on his face.

Rocket and Tuff carried her body in through the door and hit her head on the door frame on their way in. I shook my head at their carelessness, but they would never bring another woman harm.

"Man what in the entire fuck is going on?!" Animal snapped.

I turned around and glared at him. I was hoping he wouldn't get too pissed and kill them fast because I wanted to do it slow.

"Lemme holla at you." I said as I grabbed Animal's arm but he snatched away from me.

Out of reflex, I punched him in the side of his head because nobody disrespects me like that. Animal countered with a blow that dazed me slightly. I quickly shook it off and sent two blows to his stomach. Animal doubled over in pain then tackled me into the wall. The impact caused me to lose my breath but I didn't stop. I slammed my elbows into his back and it sent him down to his knees. He used his arms to grab my legs so he could pull me to the ground. We went blow for blow on the ground for at least three minutes and that was a long three minutes. "Play it cool." I said to Animal once I caught my breath. He frowned his face up at me once I extended my hand to help him up. He latched onto my hand and wiped the blood from his mouth as he got up. He nodded his head at me and we focused our attention on the fellas before us.

Juice gave Animal a head nod and I could tell it was because he thinks I'm with this shit. Razor stood off to the side with a smile on his face as if he was still amped up about the whole situation. I walked over to the girl's body and lifted her off the ground. Tuff and Rocket must have set her down while Animal and I were fighting. "C'mon Animal and Juice." I said, but didn't miss the dramatic sigh that someone let out. It wouldn't matter though because neither of them were going to leave here.

I walked all the way to the back bunker room of the warehouse. I call it the bunker room because there are six bunk beds, specifically for late or drunk nights. Ya know those nights when you may or may not make it home if you drive.

I pulled the cover back and laid her bruised body across the bed and tucked her in.
"What you doing?" Juice asked.
When I turned my body slightly, I noticed he had a confused look on his face. I shook my head at the fact that he's a street nigga and hasn't figured out that I'm not with this shit either. I know them other niggas dumb but I didn't know he was too.

"Why you in these streets man?" I asked him as I took a seat on the foot of the bed. "We'll talk later." I said as I stood up and headed out the door. I walked down the long corridor to my arsenal room. I won't explain that because the name itself is explanatory.

"Aw man." Juice exclaimed once they followed me into the room.

I grabbed my tool kit that's designed for a dentist and tied it around my waist. I looked over at Animal and he was grinning like a fat kid in the chocolate factory.

"Grab anything you need. You can have what you can carry." I said.

I'm always generous with weapons because I have a major plug. I get weapons in wholesale form by the buck and I save a lot of money doing it that way.

I watched Juice carefully as he stuck two pistols in his waistband and strapped one of them to his ankle. Once we were all strapped up, we walked back up to the front where Tuff, Rocket and Razor stood awaiting our arrival.

"Damn, I thought it would take y'all a long time. Where she at though?" Razor asked as he unfastened his belt buckle.

<u>Amber</u>

When I walked through the door of my parent's house, the look on my dad's face let me know that he already knew what happened today at school. I wasn't worried though because my parents aren't like other people's parents. See, my parents are pretty well off and they really don't pay me all that much attention and it's been that way since I was a young girl.

They have always worked long hours but there wasn't a toy that I wanted that I didn't get. There wasn't a thing I needed that I didn't have. As you can more than likely tell, I'm not missing any meals. My only problem with my parents is their complete lack of effort at being parents. It's like they think they're doing a good job because they make sure I'm taken care of and buy me whatever I want, but all a child wants is love.

I think I found love in the cookie jar because every time I started to miss them, I would eat. Pretty soon all I did was eat and that resulted in the pretty, chunky girl that I am today. Of course, you know kids are cruel and that's how I learned how to fight. I was called all kinds of names growing up and I had nobody to talk to about how those words were making me feel, so I fought whoever disrespected me.

Since I couldn't find love at home, as soon as I met Nichole when we were twelve years old, I latched onto her. It was like an instant connection and we've been best friends ever since. Well, she's been my best friend ever since. I know she looks at me the same but after five years of friendship, I just found out where she lives.

You would think that she would trust me enough to know I love her enough not to judge her. I guess I can't really blame her because she thinks I have strict parents, but I just put on a front like they care because I know they really don't.

My parents care about me about as much as her mom cares about her. Wait scratch that, I think my parents love me but her mama ain't shit. What mama gets a friend to jump their daughter? It doesn't matter what the reason is, you don't get a bitch off the street to help you jump your daughter. I hate for bitches to jump and that's why I jumped in it. Nobody is going to lay a hand on me or one of my friends because I'm going to bang behind mines, and that's on my mama. Bitches be at school talking slick about my weight like I give a fuck. I've been called every fat name known to man as a child so now, I let them words roll off my fat ass and then I punch them in their face. They may not like me, but they will respect me.

I'm loyal to a fault and I know y'all may think I'm dumb for not telling Ant's friend who she was, but it was my decision to make. When they walked in together, I already knew something was off but I didn't know what. I was not about to be the reason that Nichole got hurt. Every way I flipped the idea of just saying her name in my head, it was still my fault; so I was not about to say a word. If anything, he would kill me and still not know who she was.

"So you got into another fight?" my dad asked and it snapped me out of my thoughts. I nodded my head and sat my backpack down behind the door. "I thought you were going to stop." he said with disappointment laced in his voice.

I looked up at him with an angry look on my face because he has some nerve to be disappointed. I'm the one that was raised by a fucking nanny because my parents were always too busy for me.

"Gone bout yo business! Don't stand there and act like you care about me. What is it really? Am I making you look bad in front of your partner's down at the firm?" I asked because I knew it was somewhere along those lines.

See, my mom and dad are both lawyers and together they started their own law firm uptown. They have two other partners and together they built it from the ground up. I wasn't planned and I truly believe I only made it out the womb because my mama found out about me too late in the pregnancy to terminate it.

"Baby doll." my dad said but I cut him off by holding my hand up to his face.

"It won't happen again." I lied then stormed off to my room.

He and I both know that just as soon as something else happens that makes me feel disrespected, I'll be fighting again.

When I made it to my room I halfway expected one of my parents to come in and give me a lecture about how girls shouldn't fight or something; you know like a good parent would. I guess I wasn't considering the fact that my parents aren't the caring type. My parents care more about their image, which is why they don't take their fat daughter to those parties they throw but they brag about my 4.0 grade point average.

I started to get restless around 3 am so I snuck out of the house. Well I guess it isn't sneaking when your parents don't care. I'm sure they will only say something if I got into trouble while I was out. My heart took me straight to the place I dropped Nichole off at this morning. I remembered exactly where I was going because I've been here before.

A couple of months back, Ant was messing with this chick that lives literally in walking distance from Nichole's house. Well at the time, we were in the dating phase and I assumed we weren't dating other people. To make a long story short, we didn't have a title or even a conversation about where we were heading in our little sexcapade. So, me being the hothead that I am followed him over here one day and gave them a few minutes to get started. In all actuality, I was trying to talk myself out of it. Needless to say, I kicked the door in and started whooping both of their asses!

After I got tired, I left and didn't talk to him at all anymore until he was ready for what I was ready for. Which is what we have now. I'm almost certain he still does his thing out there, but it's kept so far in the dark that I would need more than a flashlight to find it.

I looked to the left and saw an all-black Cadillac Escalade truck turning off of the street. At first I thought it was Ant's friend Murda but it looked like a couple of people in it; and from what I hear, Murda likes to ride solo or with one other person. I shook it off and exited my car.

I was well aware that it was after 3 am as I walked up the stairs. I had no clue which door was

Nichole's door though. The only reason I knew she lived upstairs is because she has mentioned the stairs kicking her ass before at school. I stood in the hall between two doors once I reached the top of the staircase. I played eeny, meeny, miny moe until my hands stopped on the funky looking door with 143 on it. The 3 was hanging off slightly and pretty soon it would just be apartment 14. I laughed quietly to myself at the thought.

As I raised my hand to knock on the door it swung open. There stood a caramel complexioned, really pretty chick with fire red shoulder length hair. She had a weird looking tattoo of a bullet wound on her neck. Don't get me wrong whoever did it was on point with the details and she even had the blood trickling down her neck. It was oh so very hot and I bet it hurt like hell.

"Who are you?" she asked with attitude evident in her voice. "Do you know what time it is?" she asked then glanced behind her.

Before I could respond, the neighborhood hoe, Antoinette came storming towards the door. "Ain't nobody tell you to let her go bitch!" Antoinette said.

It took me a minute to figure out that these two are Nichole's sisters because none of them look alike. The one with the red hair turned around and placed her hand on her plump hip. I got a good view of her big round ass and I knew right off top that Animal would love it if I brought her home.

"Bitch yall ain't fina keep jumping on her like she's some bitch in the street! That's why I helped her leave." the redhead snapped back.

Her whole statement piqued my interest because I knew exactly who they were arguing about.

Nichole's mom and sister obviously jumped her and this redhead helped her leave. *"But where did she go?"* I thought to myself as I watched on with a confused look on my face.

"I'm glad the ungrateful bitch is gone! She thought she was better than us anyway." Nichole's mom said as she walked down the hall.

I stared at her in shock, because this is the old broad that all the dope boys be hitting on the side of the building so she could get a fix.

"Shit no wonder Nichole is embarrassed to let anyone know about her." I thought to myself.

"Who the fuck are you?" Nichole's mom asked as she squinted past her daughters.

"Chill ma." the redhead said.

"Shut the fuck up Sabrina!" her mom said and focused her attention back on me.

I took a step back because at the moment it's three against one so the deck of cards is stacked against me.

"Where did she go?" I asked Sabrina since she appears to be the only person in front of me with common sense. She shrugged her shoulders as her facial expression resembled one of someone who just watched their beloved dog get hit by a car.

I instantly felt sorry for her because I knew she was only trying to help, but she wasn't thinking clearly. Nichole doesn't know these streets and these streets don't know her. That put her in a lose-lose situation off top.

See if you don't know the streets, you won't be able to read the signs to know when you're in immediate danger. You don't know what street not to walk on or where you shouldn't sit. People take shit like sitting on the city bus bench real serious as crazy as it may sound. Nichole is a good girl, a home; body so she doesn't know these things. Since the streets don't know her or who she's related to, they're going to eat her alive. When people don't know you they try you just to see if you're bout that life. They simply want to test you out to see if you will fight; or rather or not you do drugs.

Now there's a small chance that the streets know exactly who are folks are but that would make it worse for her. The things I've heard about her mom and sister are all from bad to worst. They fucking for anything and being associated with them means you're giving the pussy up too.

"We gotta find her." I said with a worried expression on my face.
Sabrina nodded her head, but her mom came charging at me. Antoinette grabbed her mom and I think that shocked Sabrina and her mom. It didn't shock me though, because Antoinette knows I gets down. A lot of people say they are TTG (trained to go) but baby, I don't need any training. As a matter of fact, it's taking everything in me not to slap all three of these bitches right now.

"Let's go." I said to Sabrina. I didn't wait for her to respond because I was not taking no for an answer. Nichole is like a sister to me but she is her sister, so she has no choice in the matter. Before we made it down the stairs, a shoe flew over my head and hit the wall. I glanced back just to see whose ass I was going to beat after I found Nichole. I winked at her and turned back around.

As soon as we got in the car my phone started ringing. "Yea?" I answered annoyed because it was after 3 am and she should have assumed I was asleep.

"Bitch who whooped Nichole's ass like that?" Bianca asked. I looked over at Sabrina but she didn't say anything.

"Where you see her at?" I asked.

"Facebook. I'm fina send the screenshot." she said then hung her phone up. A few seconds later, I came face to face with a person I barely recognized.

Tears welled up in my eyes because of the pain she must have felt when she was being beaten so badly. "Did y'all do this?" I asked and turned the phone towards Sabrina. Her silence said it all. I backhanded her with all of my might as I drove away. Her head flew back and hit the seat as she cried.

"Weak bitches!" I mumbled to myself as my phone started to ring again. "Yea?" I answered because I was beyond pissed off at that point.

"Did you get it?" Bianca asked. I could hear people laughing about the image in the background as Bianca told them to shut up.

"Yea whose page is that on?" I asked.

"Kisha of course. She's saying she did that. She said her cousin Razor sent her the picture when he seen her but girl, she was lying in a bed on that picture. She fucking with Razor ugly lass?" Bianca asked.

I didn't respond to her, I simply hung the phone up.

"I had nothing to do with it."

Sabrina said but she didn't look at me. I didn't think she did, but I needed to hit some damn body so I didn't respond to her.

I grabbed my phone and called Ant. "What's up baby?" he answered wide awake.

"Why the fuck you up nigga?" I asked. "Nevermind fuck all that. Look, I need you to find Razor for me." I said over the phone.

"Why?" he asked.

"Nichole is missing and he was the last person to see her." I answered.

He paused for a second then told me to come to the warehouse then hung the phone up.

Nichole

I woke up and my head was pounding something serious. I laid perfectly still, as my eyes scanned the room I was in. I had no idea where I was or how I got there. All I knew was, I was in a bed alone.

As I sat up and looked around, I noticed there were other beds in the room as well. "Am I in a foster home or something?" I asked myself out loud. I stood up slowly and noticed my bag in the corner. Just to be sure it was mine, I walked up to it cautiously and looked inside. It looked as though everything was there, so I sat back on the bed.

I'm not sure how many other people are here, because all of the other beds look pretty much untouched. I looked around the room for about 15 minutes, because I was trying to build up enough courage to walk out and explore the rest of the building.

POW! The sound of a gunshot scared me and I jumped down to the floor. I threw my arms over my head like they could stop whoever had the gun from getting to me. I think I just had a mini heart attack.

My breath got caught in my throat as I slowly stood to my feet. Fear gripped my soul as I clenched the shirt I had on tightly over my chest. I approached the door slowly and held my breath as I opened it. I pulled the door open slowly so I wouldn't make too much noise as I stuck my head out into the hallway.

I walked completely out of the door and down the hall on the tips of my toes. My body still hurt like hell and I couldn't feel my face but I was alive. I continued my walk until I got to the room that I heard loud grunts coming from. I stood frozen in place in front of the open door. Shock took over fear's grip, as I watched two men being beaten. There were three guys tied to three chairs but one of them was dead. I took a step back as the memories of what happened to me took over my mind.

As I laid across the bench with a tight grip on my suitcase I could feel my eyes getting heavy. I knew it was late but I had no way of knowing what time it was, because I don't have a phone. I could feel myself drifting off to sleep and I just couldn't fight it. I don't think I even tried to fight my sleep as I slipped into a peaceful slumber.

"Look at that ass though Tuff!" I heard someone say. My eyes shot open as I looked around at the guys that stood in front of me. I knew running would be useless but I would still fight until the death of me.

"Look at her face." the guy I who assumed was named Tuff said, looking at me with a look of disdain on his face. The third guy took a step closer to me and reached out to touch my exposed thigh.

It was at that moment that I wished Sabrina had allowed me to get fully dressed before she made me leave the house. I'm sure she had good intentions but she sent me out into the lion's den with this one.

I stood to my feet with my shoebox in my hands. I knew I needed to sit it down but I desperately needed to know what was inside of it. Against my better judgement, I stood before these three guys without sitting the box down.

"What you doing out here all alone?" the guy with a cut across his face asked me. I didn't know exactly what they wanted with me but, I knew it wouldn't be anything I wanted to have done. My worst fear was that they were going to rape me.

I took a step back without answering his question. The guy that hadn't said anything yet walked around the back of the bench and gave me a hard shove. I tumbled towards the one with the cut and dropped my box in the process.

I dared not bend over and pick it up because I didn't want them focused on my body. "You don't hear me talking to you bitch?" the guy asked as he reached out and snatched my wrist. I yanked away from him but I think that pissed him off.

I kept my fist balled up at my sides as I waited for someone to make a move. The guy named Tuff took a step towards me and I swung with all of my might. The only problem is; I didn't have anything left.

As I swung, I lost my balance and fell into his arms. Someone hit me in the back of the head and all I remembered was their wicked grins before everything faded to black.

I subconsciously slid my hand between my legs but everything felt intact. I breathed a loud sigh of relief that I hadn't been raped and sent a silent prayer up to God.

"Oh Gosh Nichole!" Amber screamed. I turned around with a confused look on my face and snatched my hand out of my pants. Amber embraced me before I could explain why my hand was in my pants; or ask how she knew where I was when I didn't even know where I was.

I looked behind her as tears fell down my cheeks and they fell harder as I stared at my oldest sister, Sabrina. She mouthed that she was sorry as tears fell from her eyes as well. I know she didn't mean for any of this to happen, but I would like to know how I ended up being saved before things got out of hand with the assholes that I was with.

"C'mon let's get you out of here." Amber said.

I nodded my head as I took one last glance inside of the room. My mouth hit the floor as I stared at the man that I once had a crush on, until he tried to shoot me in the fucking bathroom after I saw him kill Pee Wee.

I didn't realize he was in there at first because my eyes were frozen on the guys seated in the chairs rather than the people who were beating them. Murda and I stared at each other and it was as if he was seeing me for the first time.

Amber grabbed my hand and tugged me roughly away from the door but Murda followed us. "Handle them." he said to a guy I had never seen before.

I gripped Amber's hand tightly and she pulled me in front of her, then turned around so she could block me from Murda's line of vision. I peeked over her shoulder at him as he looked between us. The hairs on the back of my neck stood up when he began to nod his head.

"This is her huh?" he said then smiled.

I stood as stiff as a board as I looked at him. Amber didn't budge as he took a step closer.

"Let me holla at you Nichole." Murda said in the sexiest voice I had ever heard in my life. A soft gasp escaped my lips because I had no clue he knew my name. Amber turned her head slightly to the side as she looked up at him.

"She's not going anywhere with you." Amber said. I couldn't believe she wasn't backing down from a nigga that the streets call Murda.

His name alone scares me because I know they don't call him Murda because he's nice! He has more than likely killed people! I'm far from hood and although I grew up in the hood, I'm green to the street life but even I know better than to give a nigga lip name Murda!

As much as I respect Amber for being here for me, I cannot let her get hurt because of me. I stepped from behind her and placed my hand on her shoulder.

"It's ok sis." I said then stepped in front of her.

I looked up at Murda the best I could, being as though my eyes were still very much so swollen.

"Don't." Sabrina said as Murda grabbed my wrist.

"It's ok." I looked back and said to them.

For some reason after he touched me, the fear went away. The hairs on the back of my neck laid back down and I felt safe. I didn't think any harm would come to me by following this man wherever he was going to lead me.

Murda

The funniest shit I'd seen all day was Razor's face when him and those predators realized we hadn't touched the girl. Shit, I didn't even care to make it a slow death for them anymore; just as long as they weren't alive to hurt anyone ever again. No woman should have to go through anything so traumatic and I'm extremely apologetic that she went through this to begin with.

As I stood in front of her, Amber and the chick from the old broad's house, I felt like the dumbest nigga on the planet. I looked between them and looked for any resemblance but I didn't find one, although they were both beautiful. Nichole is bright skinned, with long curly hair and although I can't see her eyes clearly right now, I now remember running into her on her way to school with those green eyes. I quickly put it together that she's also Amber's friend that saw me off Pee Wee. The missing piece right now is how she knows the other chick. She stood taller than Nichole with a caramel complexion and bright red hair.

I'll never understand why females will color their whole head like that. I mean it looks good when it's freshly done but if you don't keep it up, it looks real bad.

Anyway, I knew Amber thought I was going to hurt Nichole but I gave her my word that I wouldn't. Word is bond. Now I just need to holla at Nichole alone to read her a little bit. I was too shocked when she agreed to speak to me without me forcing her.

Hell little do Amber know, her presence is what let me know who Nichole was, because I couldn't recall.

I grabbed Nichole's arm firmly but in a gentle way if that makes sense to you. I lead her down the hall, back into the room I laid her down. I stood in front of her as she walked over to the bed and sat down on it. She stared at me briefly and I could tell she was scared because she didn't know what was or was not about to happen to her.

"What happened to you?" I asked as I looked at her. I took my time and observed the bruises and scrapes on her face. I shook my head at the mere thought of the pain she has gone through.

"I fell." she answered as she lowered her gaze to the floor. The fact that she couldn't maintain eye contact let me know that she was lying even though her answer alone was enough to know.

"Did those guys do this to you?" I asked even though I think I already know the answer.

She looked up at me with her head raised slightly as she shook her head. That let me know that it was someone she wants to either protect or get back at them herself.

"Your mom and sister did this?" I asked in a concerned tone.

Normally I don't care at all but for some reason, I actually wanted to know. I felt a strong need to save her and protect her by any means necessary. I watched tears slide out of her swollen eyes as she shook her head again. I walked close to her and squatted down in front of her as she sat on the bunk bed. I grabbed her chin and examined her face closely. My blood began to boil and I knew that her mom and sister would pay. She'd thank me later.

"I've been looking for you since you ran out of here." I said to her and watched confusion wash over her face as she frowned slightly. "When you came here with Amber, what did you see?" I asked her and she shook her head with a frown. "Did you see anything out of the ordinary?" I asked her as I looked directly in her face.

"I don't know what you are talking about." she said then gave me a light shoulder shrug. A slow smile began to spread across my face as I watched her.

"Ok." I said as I stood to my feet.

I wasn't sure if this was a stone I should leave unturned or not but I guess only time would tell. I headed towards the door so I could help Animal finish these guys off and go see ma dukes at the home.

"Aye." Nichole said so I stopped in my tracks. I didn't say anything but I did turn around to look at her. "Can I, can I um... stay here?" she asked. Man my eyes damn near bugged out of my head.

"Hell naw girl!" I said then took another step out of the door.

I heard her sigh heavily right before I made it completely out of the threshold. "You can stay with me. Let's go." I said but she didn't move.

I turned around and looked directly at her but she was still sitting in the same spot.

Shit I know she don't know a nigga but if I was going to kill her she would be dead. Hell, she's better off with me anyway because I'll never let anything happen to her. I'm sure she can go back home but how many more beatings will she have to take before she gets out on her own. Shit I'm sure this isn't the first time she had to fight her family. I walked over to her things and grabbed them then stood in front of her. She took another deep breath then stood to her feet and followed me out the door.

Before we were all the way down the hall, Amber's little humbuggish ass came power walking and met us halfway. She bypassed me and ran straight up to Nichole and began to examine her body. I'm sure she can't tell if I did anything to add to her already bruised face. Hell it really ain't even no room to add a bruise. Them bitches did a number on her.

"Did he hurt you?" I heard Amber whisper so I turned around used the wall to lean on while I watched interaction that I was sure would be quite comical.
"No." Nichole said with her head hung low. I could tell she didn't want anyone to look at her face and I don't blame her.
"You sure?" Amber asked as she grabbed her face gently to make her look up.
"Yes damn!" Nichole said as she pushed her hand away from her face.
I watched her closely as she put her head back down. I shook my head again at the fact that she's going through this.

I remember quite vividly what she looked like the day I knocked her over which was yesterday, now here she is battered and bruised. She doesn't want anyone to look at her and I can't tell if she has bags under her eyes or if that came with her getting beat the fuck up by her mama and sister.

"Listen, I need to finish up here then I'll take you home." I said as I looked at Nichole.

She nodded her head instead of responding to me. I watched Amber look back and forth between us with a deep frown on her face.

"You going back home?!" Amber all but screamed in her face.

"No." she answered softly.

"She's going to stay with me temporarily." I said and Amber's mouth hit the floor. She placed her hand on her chubby hip and walked up to me. She was so close that I could feel her body heat as she looked up at me.

"If I can't reach her, you have me to worry about. If I see her and she has one strand of hair out of place, you have me to worry about. If she misses school when we can go back-"

"I know I have you to worry about." I said in a way to cut her off. I gave her a slight smirk then glanced over at Nichole. "Keep her company while I wrap this up." I said to Amber then walked away before she had a chance to respond. I made my way back to the room that I left the guys in.

When I opened the door, Animal and Juice were both sitting down watching TV. My eyes scanned the room and I knew they hadn't done a thing since I left even though I told them to finish up.

"Took you long enough." Animal said and I gave him a low chuckle followed by a shake of my head.

"Let's get it then." I said as I rubbed my hands together.

I walked around the room looking for my dentist style belt before I realized I already had it on. I had completely forgotten that I had already put it on. I glanced over at Tuff and Rocket because Razor was already dead. For this nigga to go by the name Tuff, he sure as hell ain't tough!

I stared at this nigga in complete disbelief as he cried silently to himself. I bet he'd be sobbing real loud if he wasn't gagged. I shook my head then focused my attention on Rocket. He would be my prey and I'll leave Tuff's crybaby ass to Animal.

"Aye Juice come hold his head for me." I called out to Juice as I stood directly in front of Rocket.

Juice had a confused look on his face as he stood behind Rocket. He grabbed his head but Rocket shook his head vigorously and caused Juice to lose his grip.

"Don't fucking touch me!" Rocket snapped as he looked over his head at Juice.

I stood there with a blank expression on my face as I stared at Juice, because I was seriously trying to figure out why he's in these streets. He's clearly not made for this shit. Juice looked over at me but I knew he couldn't read my poker face. I knew one thing though, if he didn't figure out how to hold Rocket still, he was going to have me as a problem as well.

"You sold us out for what nigga?" Rocket asked as he snarled at Juice. "Cause you got a daughter? Nigga she gone be a lil hoe just like her damn mama! Bih gave me head the other night when I took her to McDonald's." Rocket said then laughed loudly.

I glanced over at Animal and he shook his head. I think Rocket is the only mufucker that found anything funny. I could look at Juice and tell his blood was finally starting to blood. I watched him closely as he closed his eyes as if he was trying to calm himself down.

"Don't!" I said in a tone that commanded attention. Juice's eyes shot open as he looked at me. "The fuck you trying to calm down for?" I asked with a slight frown on my face. "This nigga just disrespected your daughter and ole lady and what you doing about it? Counting to ten or some shit?" I asked because I was extremely disappointed.

I'd die about my respect and my respect extends to my family members. Well at least the ones I fuck with. I see now I'm going to have to take this nigga under my wing or his daughter will end up fatherless.

"Use it." I stated calmly as I continued to look at him.

Juice reared back and punched Rocket in the back of the head. Rocket's head slammed forward with so much force, that I think it broke his neck. I walked up to Rocket with a curious expression on my face until I lifted his head up.

"Damn." I said as I looked up at Juice. He had a huge smile on his face like he got real joy out of killing Rocket. "Is this your first time?" I asked and he nodded his head, then looked over at Animal. Animal gave him a look of approval. "Can you believe he hit him so hard he broke his neck?" I asked Animal with a smirk on my face.

"Sound like a major case of whiplash." Animal said and we laughed.

"Guess I gotta use my tools on Tuff then." I said as I shook my head. "And for the record nigga I wanted to kill Rocket!" I said and Animal laughed. "Nigga you always get salty when someone kill a nigga you wanted to kill." Animal said in between laughs.

"Fuck you nigga!" I said as I approached Tuff.

"Please man please don't kill me!" Tuff begged as soon as I removed the gagged.

"How did these niggas get in my fucking organization?" I questioned myself. "I'm going to kill you. You have to work with me and it won't be as bad as it could be." I explained to him as I looked down at him.

"Man I ain't even touch her man. It wasn't even my idea to grab her." he continued to plead his case.

I shook my head because at this point, it doesn't matter whose idea it was. Hell, the only thing that matters is what they were gonna do to her. He would have touched her had Razor not called me.

"Shutup nigga!" I said as I removed my cheek retractor from my belt.

"Man where you be finding this shit?" Animal asked.

"Amazon." I said in a duh like tone.

I thought everybody knew you can get anything you need for extremely low prices. Hell a nigga got a whole torture kit piece by piece off of amazon. As a matter of fact, I'm building a torture room right now!

"Aye Juice, can you come hold his head without breaking his neck?" I asked in a sarcastic way that caused Animal to laugh.

He's the funniest man you will ever meet as long as y'all are friends. If you're ever on the opposite end, you will understand exactly why we call this nigga Animal.

Juice shook his head as he side stepped towards me.
"Nigga why you walking like that?" I asked with a frown.
I know the room we're in isn't big at all but that's because this is how I wanted it. I didn't want a nigga to be comfortable when he came in here. I guess I didn't count on three niggas being in here at once plus three niggas doing the killing.

Juice didn't answer my question as he gripped the sides of Tuff's head tightly.
"Open your mouth." I said to Tuff and this nigga started crying.
I tilted my head sideways as I looked at the audacity of this nigga. All I could think about was what he was about to do to Nichole. I can only imagine how she would have been crying and begging and just like his, her pleas would have also fell on deaf ears.

I held one side of the cheek retractor in one hand and pinched the bridge of his nose with my other hand. A few seconds later, he had to open his mouth because he couldn't breathe. I stuffed one side of the retractor in and snapped it into place. Tuff's eyes got as big and as round as saucers at how swiftly I moved to insert the retractor. I grabbed the other end and repeated the same motion.
"Learn something new every day." Animal said from his position in the room.
"What?" I asked as I tried to figure out what he just learned.
"Nigga I was wondering how you was gone make the nigga open his mouth." Animal said as he shook his head. I guess it ain't common knowledge to pinch a person's nose so they can't breathe and they will open their mouth.

I remember when I was a kid and my mama use to make me eat vegetables. I would close my lips as tight as possible and turn my head away from her. One day she got tired of my shit, grabbed my nose and just held it tightly. She held it so tight that if I tried to pull away, it hurt like hell. She would hold it until I had no choice but to open my mouth and she would stuff the vegetables in my mouth. Now I could have waited until she let me go and spit them back out, but she ain't play the radio with my little ass.

Anyway, I walked away to turn my dental torch wrench on so I could test the heat levels out on it. I hadn't used it since I got it swooped up by my boy Max. Max could upgrade anything you brought his way but a whore, so I knew he would work magic on my torch. He took the torch wrench and inserted a heating needle tip.

First of all, anybody that knows what a dental torch wrench is, knows that it has no heating levels so you know Max put me on. When I powered my 2016 torch on, only the needle tip that was added would turn red. Max applied two settings to an otherwise normal dental torch, hot and blazing. When I flipped the switch to hot, the needle tip would just get extremely hot but when it's switched the blazing, it melts flesh away. I tossed Max fifteen grand to hook it up for me and since you couldn't look at it and tell it did all of that, I tossed him an extra five.

I walked over to Tuff with a big smile on my face because I've never loved anything more than killing. Of course I run the streets with an iron fist but that's my second love. Not to mention I didn't choose to do this shit. I would have been perfectly happy with being the muscle, just as long as the money was good and I could kill mu'fuckers.

Tuff was begging again but I had no idea what he was saying because of the cheek retractors. See the cheek retractors are designed to keep your mouth wide open while the dentist does shit that's so painful, you would try to close your mouth to stop him from hurting you. In my case, I use them to do shit like this.

I held the handle of the wrench tightly in my hand as I slid the needle in his gum, all the way in the back of his mouth by his wisdom teeth. He yelled out briefly as the needle pierced his skin. "Give me a face mask from under that desk." I said to Animal. He gave me a "nigga you crazy" look but got the mask and put it on for me.

"I don't know why y'all chose to rape bitches. I'd rather y'all pay for it than take something." I said as I looked at Tuff.

He had tears streaming down his cheeks and he moved his tongue around his mouth frantically as if he was trying to push the needle out.

I switched the level to hot and watched Tuff grimace in pain as he began to sob. He was trying to beg for me to stop; well at least I think that's what he was doing. I couldn't understand shit he was screaming with all this shit going on in his mouth.

A few seconds later, I pulled it out with so much force that two of his teeth came out with it. "Ew man fuck!" Juice said with his face all twisted up in disgust.

Tuff continued to cry and his mouth quickly filled with slob and blood. If he didn't swallow soon he would choke himself to death but I wouldn't mind. I stuck the needle back in but on the other side. Again

Tuff tried to speak but I still had no clue what he was trying to say.

I flipped the switch to blazing and Tuff started seizing. His ass was shaking so hard that he broke the chair and fell to the ground. He continued to shake but the wrench didn't fall out of his mouth and it was still set to blazing. It took about two minutes for the torch to burn through his gum and cheek before it fell to the floor. I reached down and picked it up then set in the washing tray. I flipped it off then noticed Tuff was still convulsing. Blood was pouring out of his mouth. I turned him over on his back as he continued to shake. He started to choke on his blood. The shakes became more rigid and his eyes bulged out his head as he took his final breath.

I reached down and checked for a pulse but he didn't have one. I pulled my gun from my waistband and fired two shots in his face just to make sure. I then went through and shot Razor and Rocket.

"I gotta take Nichole home. I'll get up with y'all." I said as I dapped them up.

"Iight bet. We gone drop the bodies off then I'll run Juice on home." Animal said as I headed out the door.

I nodded my head and walked away.

Nichole

"How did y'all end up together?" I asked Amber as I looked between her and my oldest sister Sabrina. I was really confused about their link up, as well as how they knew I was here. Amber gave me a rundown of what happened and I shook my head because I know now that they will turn their attacks on Sabrina. I know Sabrina isn't like me though and she will fight them both back. I'll fight Nette but I've never been able to bring myself to hit our mama back.

"Sabrina, do you think they will start jumping you?" I asked but she shook her head.

"Are you really gonna stay with him?" Amber asked after a few minutes of silence.

I nodded my head because I had nowhere else to go. I can't go back home and I can't make it in these streets alone. I can't go to Amber's house because she lives with her parents. It can't be that bad living with Murda, especially since I've had a crush on him for like ever and a day. I'm going to make sure I do everything I need to do so he won't put me out before I find a job.

"As soon as my face heals I'm going to find a job. Then I'll be able to find my own place so this is just temporary." I said to Amber. I glanced over at Sabrina and she had an extremely worried look on her face. "What's wrong Brina?" I asked before Amber had a chance to respond. She rolled her eyes at me but she focused her attention on Sabrina as well.

"Well that guy that you're about to live with, came in our house yesterday. Scared me half to death and threatened our lives about Pee Wee." she blurted out and shocked me.

Well I wouldn't say I was shocked because I saw him kill Pee Wee, but I'm shocked that he didn't kill them. They could easily put two and two together if the police ever find Pee Wee's body. Hopefully Murda has thought about what he's going to do in case any of that happened. If push comes to shove, I know he will kill us all in order to stay free. That's why I'm hoping it doesn't come to that. "Don't ever say that again." I said as I looked at Sabrina with a serious expression on my face.

These aren't your normal street niggas. These guys are certified and you would rather have them on your side, than going against you. I have no idea why he killed Pee Wee and I don't care because it has nothing to do with me. I'm not trying to be on his murder radar, so I'm trying to stay on his good side.

Sabrina never responded and nobody tried to make any small talk, so we were just sitting there. We sat there for a while in silence and it was the loudest thing I'd ever heard.

When I heard footsteps coming down the hall, I peeked out of the room.
"That's ya problem right there ma. You nosey as hell." Murda said.
The way his voice boomed off the wall scared me so bad I damn near jumped out of my skin. Amber laughed softly and I shot her a look. I was super glad she wasn't making any comments about my face because I'm real insecure right now.

"Let's go." Murda said to me.

I stood up quickly and he grabbed my things. I followed him out the door and to his truck. Instead of getting in right away, I walked up to him and began to lift his shirt up. "Hold up ma what the hell you doing?" he asked as he used his arm to push me away gently. The gesture killed my ego as I looked up at him.

"You have blood all over this shirt. You should drive with your shirt off instead of wearing a bloody shirt." I explained as I continued to stare at him.

"Get in." he said then turned his back to me.

For some reason, disappointment washed over my body as I walked around to the passenger side of the truck. I'll forever be grateful that he's giving me a place to stay, even though it is temporary. I've survived with my family this long, so I'm sure I can co-exist with Murda until I find a spot of my own.

I'd love to go off to college somewhere but I don't really like school or have the money to go. I guess if I study harder and get better grades, I could get in somebody's school or at least get a trade or something. I sat in the passenger's seat of Murda's truck extremely disappointed about the life I've lead.

I never knew my daddy and my mama has never loved me. Sabrina is the only one that has ever halfway cared, but even she never fooled with me. Everything I've learned is stuff I picked up from Amber at school. Hell if it wasn't for Amber, I wouldn't know what to do when my period came on. I remember it like it was yesterday.

We were in the 7th grade and the bell had just sounded, which indicated that our first period class had ended. My stomach had been hurting really bad all day and I had no idea what was wrong. I had asked my mom if I could stay home from school but she said she would be busy all day and didn't want to look in my face.

I waited until everyone was gone except for Amber, although I didn't know her at the time. I stood up slowly and I got scared when it felt like I had pissed on myself. My breath got caught in my throat and I stuck my hand between my legs and saw blood. Tears began to stream down my face at a rapid pace.

"Girl what's wrong with you?" Amber asked. I looked up slowly and she rushed over to me with a frown on her face. When she saw the blood on my hand, she turned her nose up in disgust. "Yo period on girl, what you crying for?" she asked. She shook her head and took her sweater off.

I stared at her in confusion until she tied the sweater around my waist. "Will your mama come get you?" she asked as she grabbed my wrist and pulled me towards the door. I shook my head and she turned to get her purse and book bag.

I didn't say a word as she led me to the girl's locker room. I didn't play anything and from her size I knew she didn't either, so I had no idea why we were in the locker room. I watched closely as she rummaged through people's clothes until she found a pair of pants and panties. I almost freaked out when she stuffed the items in her book bag and walked out of the locker room.

She led me to the bathroom and pushed me inside of the last stall. "Lucky for you girl my cycle is about to come on, so I have an extra pad in my purse. Take your pants and panties off." she said. I didn't move, I just stood there and looked at her with a strange look on my face.

"C'mon now girl, you gone have us late." she said as the bell sounded, so we knew we were late. If you go to class tardy, they will call your parents and I did not want them to call my mama. "Shit." she said as she walked out of the stall.

I heard water running and when she returned, she had wet paper towels that she put hand soap on. I would have never thought to do that. I quickly pulled my clothes down, wiped myself clean and threw the paper towels in the toilet.

She handed me the panties but I turned my nose up at her. "Beggars can't be choosers." she said with a smirk, but I still didn't move. "Girl the pad gone be on the line, so ya lil cat won't touch it." she explained. I grabbed the panties and stepped into them one leg at a time.

Amber handed me the pad but I didn't know what to do with it. "This ya first period?" she asked and I nodded my answer. "Damn, ya moms ain't tell you shit huh?" she asked but I didn't answer her because it was clear. Amber showed me how to put the pad on then we left campus. Shit, we been tight ever since.

"Do you hear me talking to you?" Murda asked with a frown on his face.
"Huh?" I asked confused as I looked over at him.
"What you want to eat?" he asked without taking his eyes off the road.
I shrugged my shoulders because I don't know how much money he has or what I can order or nothing.

I don't know much about Murda other than he has this truck and he runs shit. Hell, I don't even know exactly what he runs. I don't run the streets or hang out, so I'm never around anyone to gossip or get the latest but I'm fine with that.
I glanced over at Murda as he drove. I admired his smooth brown skin. He had a tattoo that traveled around his neck of what looked like a dragon. It was upside down and since he had his shirt off, I could tell the dragon blew fire on his back. It was the weirdest but cleanest tattoo I had ever seen. I think my sister Sabrina got him beat on the weird scale with her tattoo of the bullet wound though. I've always wondered why she got that but never got around to asking. Maybe if we had the kind of relationship sisters should have, I would have been able to ask her by now.
About fifteen minutes later, we pulled up to Bay's Seafood. I had never heard of this restaurant before but as I've said, I don't run the streets or get out much.
"Are you allergic to anything?" Murda asked as he pulled up to the drive thru.
I shook my head to answer his question.

"Fish or shrimp?" Murda asked, but I think I didn't answer him fast enough because he ordered my platter mixed with both. You know my extra hungry ass wasn't complaining though.

Before we got to the window, I pulled the rubber band out of my hair so my hair would fall freely and cover my face. I didn't want anyone to see me looking like this. I haven't even been looking at myself since we got in the truck. I haven't even looked out the window because I feared what I may look like.

I could feel Murda's intense gaze on me but I refused to look up. He had already seen enough. I heard him suck his teeth, then I smelled the food. My stomach started growling immediately and embarrassed the mess out of me. He chuckled lightly as he pulled off.
"Are they open 24 hours a day?" I asked because the sun was just starting to shine brightly.
"Hmm mmh." Murda said as he drove like a bat out of hell.
I clenched the door handle as we rode about 15 minutes and pulled up to the nicest house I had ever seen in my entire life. It looked like a baby White House and was even painted all white. There was one of those bench swings in the middle of the front yard that was also painted white. We pulled up to the gate and Murda pressed his pinky finger against a slot that opened, after he entered his pin code. "Darnell." he said after a picture of an ear flashed across the screen. I looked away quickly once Murda looked in my direction.

We pulled up in his circular driveway and parked directly in front of the house. "Grab the food." Murda said as he hopped out and grabbed my garbage bag. I was completely embarrassed about my whole situation.

When I walked in the house and closed the door I heard a beep. I looked around for Murda and when I spotted him, he was entering a code then he placed his ring finger in the finger spot. "Secured." the automatic system stated. I smiled because I was in awe. I slipped out of my shoes because I wanted to see what the smooth looking all black marble floors felt like under my feet. Murda didn't tell me where to go or what to do so I walked around until I found the kitchen.

The kitchen had all black appliances with an island counter that I fell in love with instantly! I sat his plate in the oven and sat mine on the counter. I opened the refrigerator and was shocked that it was fully stocked. I don't think I've ever in my 17 years of living, seen a refrigerator fully stocked. There were so many options to choose from that I didn't know what to choose. I settled on a sprite and some wine later, if it's ok with Murda.

I sat at the counter and demolished my entire plate in less than five minutes. I had no idea Murda was standing in the doorway until I burped on my way to trashcan. He laughed at me and there I stood embarrassed yet again.

"Excuse me." I said softly. I rolled my eyes but I'm sure he couldn't tell as puffy as they were.

"Did you drink all of your drink?" he asked and I shook my head. He handed me three pills and I looked at him crazy. "One is for swelling. One is for pain. One is for nausea." he explained.

"I'm not nauseous." I said to him with a confused look on my face.

"You will be after you take the one for pain." he said with a slight smirk on his face.

I threw all caution to the side because if he was going to do anything to me, he would have done it already. I threw all three pills in my mouth and used the rest of my drink to wash it down.

Murda

"C'mon I ran you some bath water." I said to Nichole with my hand extended. She looked a bit hesitant at first, then she placed her small hand in the palm of mine. I shocked myself by running her a bath because I have never done anything like that in my life. Hell, no woman has ever even been here before. I kind of felt like I owed her one since my workers grabbed her and were about to rape her. I went all out too.... lit candles around the tub and everything so she could relax. I even poured bath beads in the tub, which I was shocked was still in there from when I tried to take care of my mom. By the way, it proved to be impossible because I didn't trust anyone to come in my home and take care of her, so she was pretty much being neglected.

Anyway, whenever I'm dealing with a female it's solely for sex and we can do that at their place, then I'll bring my ass home. Before you think it, no I've never been hurt. I've just always been about my money. Now when I'm ready to settle down I will, but I won't know until I meet someone that makes me want to settle down. In all actuality, it could have been Nichole, since she got me wanting to take care of her already; but she's young as hell. I don't even know how old she is, but I know she's in high school so I'm not even about to fuck with her like that. I'm just going to help her in her time of need until she gets on her feet then she has to go.

I've done a lot of shit that should have landed me in prison and I'm a free man, so I'm not about to let some young pussy send me under the jail. Then on top of that, niggas with charges like that get targeted, so I'd just die in jail because I'm not about to let anyone touch me.

"Is there another bathroom or something?" Nichole asked and snapped me out of my thoughts. I looked back at her and realized I had passed the bathroom right on up.

"My bad ma." I said as I walked her inside of the bathroom.

I looked back at her and her mouth was wide open. "Was that girl your sister or y'all live in the same building or what?" I asked because I hadn't figured out how she ended up with Amber yet.

"That's my sister. We live together." she answered with her head hung low. It let me know that it's too soon to pry. I thought females like to vent but I guess she doesn't.

"Everything you need is in this closet right here." I said to her as I opened the bathroom closet door. I kept everything stocked because I don't like running out of anything I may need. I closed the bathroom door behind me and left out of the bathroom.

I walked into the kitchen because I was hungry too, but I didn't know where she put my plate. "I know she ain't eat mine too." I said out loud to myself as I looked in the refrigerator. I checked the microwave, then the oven and found my plate. I didn't realize how hungry I was until I started eating. All I ordered for me was a catfish sandwich and fries. I washed it down with a Lime-A-Rita and headed to my room to take a shower. It was super early in the morning but this is really the only time I sleep. I'm normally out and about all night long so I sleep in the mornings. I laid down and fell straight to sleep after my shower. I was knocked out, until the alarm on my phone went off.

It was Saturday morning at 9am and my mom still loves all blues Saturday so I got up, got dressed and headed out of my room. I checked each room on my way through the house but I didn't see Nichole. I stopped at the bathroom door and knocked but I got no answer. I wasn't trying to see her naked, so I opened the door slowly and peeked inside and she wasn't there. I walked all the way inside the bathroom and checked the closet but she wasn't there. She cleaned up after herself so it didn't look like she was ever there.

I left out of the bathroom and was about to head out the door when I saw her asleep sitting on the couch. She didn't even have the TV on. She had on one of my T shirts and it swallowed her small frame completely. I couldn't tell if the medicine started working for swelling or not, because I knew it would look a lot worse before it started to look better. I walked up close to her and scooped her body up in my arms. I was going to let her sleep in the guest room that's directly across from my room in case she needed me or something.

I laid her body in the queen sized bed and tucked her in. The medicine for pain had her completely out of it, because she didn't wake up at all as I positioned her comfortably in the bed. I shook my head and wrote her a note then left.

On my way to the home, I contemplated giving up the street life so I could take care of my mama at home. The doctor told me she won't be so out of it if she had people coming around her more to show her that she's still loved.

As I told you before, one of my enemies tortured her and now she has no legs. Well, she still has legs but they're prosthetic legs. Lately she has been refusing physical therapy, so her health is deteriorating again. She won't eat or nothing so today I'm going to try and talk some sense into her.

When I pulled up to the home, I powered my phone off like I do every time I come see her. If my dad or uncle needs me and I don't answer, they know to call the home. As far as my workers, they can call Animal.

I walked in, signed in and proceeded down the hall to my mother's room. When I opened the door, she sat in a wheelchair with her back to the door as she gazed out of the window.

"You want to go outside?" I asked and just like always, she didn't respond.

Sometimes I wonder if she blames me because I blame myself and maybe that's why she won't talk to me. I don't come see her that often but I come as much as I can. Her hair is thinning out so I know they aren't taking care of it but that's not a part of the package, so I guess I can't complain about something like that. She's also losing a lot of weight.

"C'mon ma let's go outside it's all blues Saturday." I said, as I wheeled her out of the building.

We went out the back door and out to the picnic area. I pulled my phone out, powered it back on and played the station that plays nothing but blue's music on Saturday, 104.1, with my IHeartRadio app.

My mother smiled brightly as her favorite song came through the speakers. I bet she wished I had turned the radio on about thirty seconds ago so she could hear it from the beginning. She smiled and snapped her fingers to the beat of Mel Waiters "Hole in The Wall."

"I took my high class woman
with me the next night
She didn't want to get out of the car
She said it didn't look right
She walked into the room
with her nose in the air
It's 7 in the morning y'all
She's still in there
Smoke filled room
Whiskey and chicken wings
People dancing and drinking
and no one wants to leave
let's go baby to the hole in the wall
I've had my best time y'all at the hole in the wall"

I sat at the table the entire time the song was on and watched my mom smile and sway to the music with her eyes closed. I can only imagine what she was thinking about and I can guarantee you it's my dad. He and I had it out after the incident happened, but not because of whose fault it was. We got into it because he stuck her in this home and haven't come to see her not even once. Nigga talking about he can't stand the sight of her because it hurt too bad. That was the most selfish thing I had ever heard in my life.

Nichole

When I woke up, I didn't want to move because it felt like I was laying on top of a cloud. I knew Murda laid me in this bed because after my awesome bath, I made my way back to the living room. I expected him to be in the living room waiting on me, ya know so he could give me a tour and let me know what's off limits; but he didn't do any of that. I ended up falling asleep right where I sat. I want to call him inconsiderate so bad, but the fact that he thought enough of me to put me in this bed erased that completely out of my head.

I sat up slowly so I could take in the room. There were three dressers that were dark brown with a red tint. There was a tall one in the corner, a wide one directly in front of the bed with a mirror and the short one was next to the bed with a lamp on it.

I climbed out of bed a little groggy from the pain medicine but I didn't want to lay around all day. I ran my hand across the foot of the bed and felt the smooth wood that was the same color as the dresser. The comforter set was black, as was the sheets and pillow cases. The room had two windows that had black curtains over them. I walked up to each window and opened the curtains to allow the sun to shine in but he had wooden blinds. That was by far the weirdest thing I had ever seen. I pulled the string on the blinds to open them so the natural light could fill the room.

I stood at the window and looked at the pool in the backyard. It was a pretty big pool, had lounge chairs all around it and two canopies for shade. I smiled to myself as I pictured this being my home, and that being my pool as I hosted pool parties every weekend during the summer.

I turned away from the window so I could finish looking at my temporary room. I made my way over to a door and when I opened it, I knew it would be called a walk in closet but it was big enough to park a car in. It was completely empty and I knew that once I started hanging my things up, it would still be completely empty.

There was another door next to it so I opened it, walked in and realized I have a bathroom in my room. I smiled brightly and started to jump up and down. I Whipped and Nae Nae'd then hit the shmoney dance in the middle of the bathroom floor. It wasn't as big as the other bathroom but it was just right for me.

After sharing one bathroom with three women, you know I'm not picky at all. Hopefully Murda lets me decorate my room and bathroom, because all of this black is a bit depressing. The toilet cover, mat in front of the toilet and tub mats are all black. The shower curtain and toothbrush holders are both black.

I walked out of my room and headed back to the living room to get my things. When I saw the bag, I opened it to make sure my shoe box was still inside of it, then dragged it all the way back to my room.

By the way, that marble floor that I was telling you about covers every room that I've been in so far. It looks so smooth though and nice too! There aren't any scuff marks anywhere or anything. I can only imagine running through this house and busting my ass if I have socks on! Ha! Now that's a sight to see.

After I put my things in my room, I made the bed and walked back out to the kitchen. I used the ice maker to put ice in a bag so I could put it on my face to help the swelling. I was extremely ready to see normally again but even more ready to look like myself.

I sat the bag of ice on the dresser and dumped all of my clothes on the bed. I folded all of my shirts, put them up, then hung my pants up. I sank down low when I realized I only have three pairs of panties and one pair of shoes. I was about to look and feel a hot mess and in three days, I'd be walking around with a bare booty.

Once I put everything away, I threw the trash bag away and hopped on my bed with the shoebox. I opened it slowly and carefully because I had no idea what was in it. As I stared at the contents of the box, I was a bit confused. It was filled with unopened envelopes. I poured them all out on the bed and noticed they had Happy Birthday on it, but each one corresponded with a different birthday. I rummaged through them until I saw the envelope that said "Happy First Birthday" with Nichole Jackson and my mom's address written underneath it.

I ripped the letter open and tears flooded my eyes. I stared at a picture of this man holding a newborn baby girl. I knew it was my dad and I before I ever read the back of the card. "Nicholas Perez." I said out loud to myself. We took the picture the day I was born, May 7th, 1999. Hot tears streamed down my cheeks as I read the letter:

"Happy 1st Birthday baby girl! I'm so sorry I wasn't there to celebrate with you, but it's only to

protect you. I've missed your first word. I missed you learning how to crawl. I missed you pulling up on things so you could learn how to walk...and I missed your first step. I know you're not old enough to understand right now, but hopefully one day you will forgive me for my absence. I'm watching you. Love Dad."

I used the sleeve of Murda's shirt to wipe my eyes as I stuck the letter back in the envelope, but there was a smaller one inside of it. I took it out and placed it inside of the shoe box. I guess I'll read all the letters first then see what's in the other envelope if there's one in all of them. I put the first letter in the short dresser's top drawer and closed it up.

I ripped open the second birthday envelope:

"Happy 2nd Birthday baby girl! Man time is flying and I cannot wait to meet you! You are as gorgeous as ever! It's killing me to watch you go through what you're going through, but it will all be worth it. I love you! Dad."

I sat the letter in the nightstand confused then peeked inside of the envelope and saw another one so I put it in the shoebox.

"Happy 3rd Birthday baby girl! You are getting so big mi amor! Those green eyes are going to break hearts! I got my shotgun ready! I love you! Dad."

By the tenth happy birthday letter I was no longer sad, I was pissed off. My dad was supposed to protect me but he has watched me go through everything that I've been through my entire life and has done nothing to help me! How can you stand there and watch your child get beat by her mother and sister; and do nothing to help? He stated just as clear as day in one of the letters that it was taking everything in him not to kill my mama.

Now I'm like, why would you stand back and watch that happen to your daughter? He said he stayed away to keep me safe but he has always watched me from a distance and knew everything that I was going through. I couldn't read anymore letters. I stuck the remaining seven in the shoe box and slid the shoebox underneath the bed. I laid back against the bed and closed my eyes as I poured out another freestyle from my heart.

"It's a travesty how words can be so sweet. Hours turns into days and days turned into weeks. My life is not the dream that I envisioned in my sleep. My father's not the man that I envisioned him to be. Am I asking for much, when I just happen to touch. This DNA that we share that you ain't crafted in months!"

"AAARRGGGH!!!!" I screamed out in frustration. I couldn't concentrate and normally freestyling alone is how I release pent up frustration. What am I gonna do? I shouldn't have opened the box. Why did Sabrina have it any damn way? I need to get back over there to find out some much needed answers to my questions.

Amber

I didn't go home after Nichole and Murda left, because I didn't feel like hearing my parents mouth. I knew the song and dance all too well, so I would just have to ride around until they both left for work. Either that or just go to Ant's house that he lets me stay in whenever I need to.

"You think she's going to be ok?" Sabrina asked.

I looked at her crazy because I forgot that she was with me. I nodded my head and turned the music up. I love Nicki Minaj because she's so different and she embraces that. I rapped along with her lyrics to the song by her featuring Ciara called "I'm Legit."

"I'm like really famous, I got a famous anus
No, not Famous Amos, all this fame is heinous
Lemme, lemme hear that boy, lemme, lemme wear that boy
All this money coming in, but I never share that, boy
No lipstick, no lashes though
But I got a real big ole ratchet, though
I said dude, yo dude, you packing dough
He said he want a good box like Pacquiao
I said, "Well, my name Nicki and it's nice to meet you."
If you really wanna know, I'll give you my procedure
Got a whole bunch of pretty gang in my clique
And we looking for some ballers, alopecia
I hate wack niggas, I should really slap niggas
These niggas tripping when I put 'em on the map niggas

How you gone break fly? How gone fake die?
Ain't at no wedding but all my girls cake, ha!
Sleeping on me, no mattress though
I'm a burn the beat down, no matches though
No they can't keep up? They molasses slow
I'm the greatest Queen bitch, with the cashes flow
Looking at me like it's my fault
Trying to sneak pictures with they iPhone
I like independent bitches like July 4th
Now that's what young Harriet died for"

I was so into the verse that I didn't notice Sabrina staring at me until the hook came back on.
"What bitch?" I asked with my face twisted up.
"I guess you really like Nicki huh? Bitch you were making her faces and everything that's why I was looking at you." she said and it caused me to laugh at her.
I could tell she was starting to loosen up now that she knows her sister is ok, but I don't want her to get shit twisted. We ain't friends and just to show her we ain't, I'm taking her ass back home.
The first chance I got to turn around, I did and headed straight back to the apartments she lived in with her mom.
"Oh gosh I need a job as soon as possible so I can get out of here." Sabrina said after we pulled up to their place. I thought about it for a second then picked up my phone to make a call.
"What's up ma? I'm a little busy right now." Ant said instead of just saying hello.
I knew exactly what he was doing because I saw the guy tied down to the chairs and heard the gunshots before Murda came to get Nichole from us.

"I got a driver for you. She's desperate and needs to get out her mom's place." I said quickly so I wouldn't hold him up too long. The last thing I need is for my guy to get caught off guard by the folks with bodies on him.

"Who?" He asked. I could hear that other guy talking in the background but I couldn't hear what he was saying.

"Sabrina. Nichole's sister." I answered him.

"You vouching for her?" he asked. I cut my eyes over at her for a few seconds then told him I did and disconnected the call.

"He's going to find you when he needs you. All you gotta do is drive." I said to her and she smiled brightly then hopped out of my car.

I shook my head and pulled off. I hope like hell she's ready to haul drugs across state lines because I don't want to have to kill my best friend's sister.

I'm not going to tell her why she's driving and hopefully Ant won't either. The last girl, Tiffany, I sent his way did just fine until she found out she was hauling cash there and drugs back. Her very next trip she got pulled over. I had to hurry up and get arrested so I could kill her.

I almost didn't make it to that city's jail in time because she was about to be transported out the following morning. I never want to have to do that again. My parents chewed me a new asshole but somehow got me out and got my record expunged. The only person that knows about why I actually went is Ant.

The ringing of my phone interrupted my thoughts as I glanced at the screen.

"Do this bitch ever sleep?!" I said out loud as I hit the button to answer it.

"Bitch did you find out what happened?" Bianca's ghetto voice blared through my car's speakers.

I rolled my eyes and sighed heavily. I have no idea why she talks to Nichole if she doesn't really like her. That shit beats the hell out of me for real. There's nothing more dangerous than having a best friend that really doesn't like you. Bianca probably only talks to her to get in her business, but Nichole don't share any information about herself so she's mad.

I know she's glad that Nichole got hurt so she can have something to talk about. Had I saw the picture on Facebook, I would have snapped out on the bitch but I bet Bianca's ass was egging it on.

Bianca and I have been friends longer than Nichole and I. I remember how I met them both. As for Nichole, I'm sure you already know but to make a long story short, her period came on at school and I helped her. Now with Bianca, there's no way in hell to make the story short.

I walked into Ms. Peterson's first grade class with my lunchbox in hand. All of the other kids called me fat instead of Amber and it really hurt my feelings. It took a really long time for me to say anything back but whenever I did, nobody laughed. It was like me being called fat was the biggest joke and the funniest thing they ever heard, so they would laugh super hard at me. Then I would try to jank back and everybody would just stare at me then burst into a fit of laughter together, but I knew they were laughing at me.

When at home, I constantly begged my parents not to make me go to school, but they didn't care about the other kids bullying me. My mom told me what to tell them next time I went to school and I couldn't wait to get there the next day.

"Boom. Boom. Boom." Bianca said for each step I took in the classroom. Everyone started laughing and pointing at me. "Fee. Fi. Fo. Fum." Cedric said, as if I was as heavy as a giant. "I'm rubber your glue, whatever you say to me bounces off of me and sticks to you!" I said back to Cedric. "Yeah a big, big, bouncy rubber ball!" he said and everyone started laughing.

Tears streamed down my cheeks as I stood in front of the class as everyone laughed. I looked at Ms. Peterson for help, but she pretended like she hadn't heard a thing, just like she does every day. I knew teachers were supposed to protect me at school but this one wasn't doing that. She didn't laugh with the other kids but she didn't stop them either.

I walked right up to Cedric and punched him square in the mouth as hard as I could. He didn't even hit me back, he just started crying. "Ooooh!" Bianca said as she pointed at what I had just done. "Go big girl! That's my big girl!" Bianca sang and dance.

She walked up to me and grabbed my hands to dance with me, until Ms. Peterson separated us and lead me out the door. We were heading towards the principal's office when Ms. Peterson fell forward and hit the floor. I looked behind us and noticed

Bianca had come out and tripped Ms. Peterson so I could get away.

Together we ran out of the doors of the school to the playground in the backyard. That was the start of an awesome friendship.

"Helllllluuuurrrr!" Bianca screamed in my ear.
"Oh shit girl I forgot I was on the phone!" I exclaimed. I had zoned completely out and was just driving and thinking. I had even passed my turn to go to Ant's house.
"Bitch fuck all that! What happened? I know you know." she said and I shook my head.
"I don't know." I said.
      I had never talked about either of my friends behind their backs and I'm not going to start now. If she wants to know what happened to Nichole, whenever she sees her she needs to ask her. Hell I hadn't even had a chance to tell Nichole that Razor took a picture of her and it's on Facebook. I need to tell her before we go back to school.
      I hung the phone up on Bianca and called Ant back.
"What baby?" Ant answered out of breath.
"Damn what I do?" I asked.
"I told you I was busy what's up?" he said and I could tell he was trying to calm his nerves. He knows I will snap out on his ass.
"What's Murda number so I can talk to Nichole?" I asked and heard him suck his teeth. I smiled at his jealousy but now is not the time.
"Baby I'm not giving you his number." he said to me. "Grab the legs." he said to someone else and I could hear him grunting.

I waited until he stopped moving before I continued. "I just need to talk to Nichole." I explained.

"Murda be on the go. She probably at his house by her damn self right now." Ant said then started laughing. I rolled my eyes and immediately felt bad for her.

"Where he live?" I asked and he laughed harder.

"Even if you knew, you wouldn't be able to get in. She can't even get out." he said and my mouth hit the floor.

"He's holding her prisoner?" I asked. I had to pull my car over so I wouldn't wreck.

"Naw but he locks up when he leaves and nobody knows the code to get in and out but him." Ant said. I threw my head back against the headrest and slapped the steering wheel.

I gripped the steering tightly and screamed because I was beyond frustrated. "Calm down. Listen." he said but I didn't respond. "Baby?" he called out.

"Yeah." I answered with my head laying on the steering wheel.

"I'm going to call him for you and have him buy her a phone." he said and I felt joyous once again. "Ok baby! Thanks bye!" I said then hung up the phone.

Anthony (Animal) Taite

"Man I don't know what the hell I'm going to do with her." I said to Juice after Amber hung the phone up. She had already called me twice before we finished doing what we were doing which is, disposing of bodies. I got her little ass spoiled, so I know it's my fault. Shit, I just be trying to make shit hard on the next nigga if he tries to slide in. Plus, Amber's young ass is crazy as hell too; and that's how I like them! She's beautiful though, so I've always looked past every flaw she thinks she has. When I first met her she used to call herself fat all the damn time, and it pissed me off because I think she's sexy. I needed her to have confidence in her appearance and she finally does.

"Sound like you got ya hands full." Juice said as he grabbed Tuff's legs. We had already dumped Razor's body on the side of the road and now we were getting rid of Tuff.
"Shit you and me both right?" I asked as I grabbed Tuff under his arms to lift him up. We didn't even get off the truck to dump his body. We swung him back and forth and let his legs go on three.
"Yeah man. Rocket kind of got in my mental." Juice answered as he hopped off the side of the truck.
I hopped off the other side and climbed back in the driver's seat. "Kind of?" I asked as I cranked the truck up and pulled off.
Juice sighed heavily and stared out the window for a few minutes. We rode in silence until I found another spot to leave Rocket's body.

"Don't spit on him or nothing." I said then climbed out of the truck so I can get on the back of it with Rocket's body.

Juice nodded his head and grabbed Rocket's legs. I watched him dig through his pocket until he found Rocket's trap phone. He flipped it open then stuck it in his pocket. I shook my head because he was about to find some shit out I'm sure he wouldn't be able to handle.

We tossed Rocket's body and left. I drove around aimlessly as Juice went through Rocket's phone. I shook my head because he was going to find some shit out that would make him want to kill that damn girl. Well I don't know for sure, but I know when you go looking for shit you usually find it.

I grabbed my phone and called Murda before I forgot to relay Amber's message.
"What's up?" he answered.
"Aye you ain't with moms?" I asked because he normally goes to see her on Saturday's.
"Yea man just left what's up?" he asked and I could tell something must have gone wrong with his visit. That's the only time he talks shitty after seeing her.
"Did you think about getting Nichole a phone or did you just leave her?" I asked even though I knew the answer already. If she had a phone I'm sure she would have already called Amber.
"Tell yo girl to mind her damn business. I'mma stop on my way back. I'm fina head that way now." he said and I laughed.
"Iight bet." I said then hung the phone up.

When I glance over at Juice, he had a spaced out look in his eyes. I looked down at his hand and he gripped Rocket's phone tight as fuck. I could see his knuckles turning ashy. His eyes were red and I could tell he was clenching his teeth.

"Take me home." Juice said to me without looking at me.

"Naw bruh. You fina kill baby mom's man. You gotta think about your daughter for a minute." I said.

It felt weird with me being the voice of reason but somebody gotta do the shit. Hell Rocket's already dead but if he wasn't, I'd let him kill him. You just can't kill the mother of your child though.... especially not for cheating.

"Take me home." he repeated.

I could tell he was fighting back tears and in all honesty, I'd kill the bitch too and chop her body up and feed it to the pigs but that's just me.

This nigga Juice ain't built like me. He's cut from a different cloth. A softer, more gentle cloth. The kind of fabric that will make him kill himself after he kills her and that will just leave the baby parentless and I can't have that shit.

"Naw nigga. If you go there now, you gone beat the shit out of her. What you need to do is just cut her ass off. Find you a bitch that looks way better than her and that's on her shit." I said then he nodded his head as he looked at me. "Boss up on her and make her wish she never cheated my nigga." I said and he continued to nod his head.

"You right man. I can't go there tonight." he said as he shook his head and began to stare out of the window.

"You can stay at one of my cribs. Monday I'll scoop you up and take you to go get your own crib and a whip. You gotta stunt on her man." I explained because I know how the shit goes.

"In my last relationship, I started off cheating on her. Where she messed up at is she forgave me for it the first time, so I knew she would again. If you cheat on a chick in the beginning and she don't drop you like a bad habit, you can bet your last dollar that she will forgive you again. Anyway, I kept cheating but I never cheated with the same chick. Eventually, she got tired of me cheating on her but she still didn't leave, so I kept doing me. Man it took everything in me not to kill her when I found out she had started doing her too. Cheating is what niggas do not women, so for a woman to cheat, it means she ain't shit! She probably had been cheating all along but hey, what's done is done right? So man, I dropped her ass like it wasn't nothing. I started making more money and buying more houses. When she saw my first new whip she tried to get me back, but you ain't gotta cheat on me but one time for me to know I've had enough. She wasn't about to keep getting out on me." I said to him.

When I looked over at him, he was looking at me crazy. "What nigga?" I asked as I looked between him and road.

"I never cheated on her man." he said as he shook his head again.

"Well then you stumbled across a bitch that ain't shit. How long y'all been together?" I asked after he crossed his arms across his chest.

"Nine years." he stated as he shook his head again. Shit, I shook my head too. I bet it sucked to be in a relationship with a hoe.

I didn't even know she had a nigga until I met Juice, that's just how much she gets down. Hell I didn't even know she had a child.

"Damn man yea just let her go." I said as I drove to one of my extra houses.

    When we pulled up, I tossed him the keys. "Make yourself at home. Well not home, home. Nigga don't mess my crib up. I'll be back Monday." I said to him. He laughed and shook his head then climbed out of the truck.

"Where you headed?" he asked as he looked at me.

"Wash the back of the truck out." I answered.

"Shit I could have rode with you." he said.

"Naw nigga you depressing me and shit. You know misery loves company but I got shit to do." I said seriously and he laughed.

"I appreciate this man." he said and I nodded my head then pulled off.

Murda

I tried as hard as I could to get my mom to talk to me, but she wouldn't budge. I kept my phone on and I played her song over and over with hopes that she would say something to me, but she never did. I didn't stop playing it until tears started streaming down her face. I didn't want to leave her like that but I'd be back real soon and hopefully she felt better.

I stopped and talked to the doctor and he explained that if she doesn't start getting nourishments in her body on her own that they would have to force her by inserting a feeding tube. I didn't want that to happen, but if she wouldn't comply on her own then they had my blessing to do what was needed to insure she lived.

I had completely forgotten about Nichole until Animal called me. Shit, I can't believe I'd left her in the house alone all day without at least a phone to use. Hell I'm sure everybody her age has a Facebook page, so if she had a phone I'm sure she would be online looking at something.

I added into my plans to go find her a phone and take it to her but I needed to check on my traps first. I always did random pop ups to insure everyone was on their shit at all times. I didn't have time for niggas to get caught slipping and I end up losing product.

I zoomed through the hood until I stopped at Boobie's trap house. I parked a few houses down and hopped out of my truck to walk the rest of the way. I watched closely as a smoker knocked on the door. It opened and the smoker walked in. I stopped in my tracks and waited for about five minutes then proceeded to the door.

I knocked and Boobie answered the door with a huge grin on his face.

"What's up nigga?" he asked as he let me in.

"Can't call it." I replied as I walked all the way in. The TV in the living room was on but nobody was watching it.

I walked into the living room and Bull was playing the overseer. He stood guard over the smokers as they got high and Brains escorted them out the back door. I nodded my approval and left.

On my way out the door, I carefully studied my surroundings because I was not about to get caught slipping. Once I made it to my truck and pulled off, I called Skip.

"What's up?" Skip answered. I could hear wind blowing so he must have been outside.

"Where you?" I asked.

"On the South Side." he answered.

The wind got louder so I pulled the phone away from my ear. "How shit looking right now?" I asked.

"I can't tell if he's doing anything out the ordinary but I'll keep you posted." he said then disconnected the call.

In case you forgot, I got Skip following Toto to see if we need to off him or let him make it. I guess we will figure it out in due time just like everything else.

I drove by Red's trap house and shook my head in disappointment. It wasn't nothing to kill them over, but they can't have bitches hanging out on the porch with them. I picked up my phone to call him and he answered on the third ring.

"Get them bitches gone." I stated calmly. I watched him look around like he was trying to figure out where I was. "Now!" I bellowed through the phone.

"I gotcha." he said.

I focused my attention on the porch as I watched the bitches scatter like roaches when you turn the light on.

I pulled off and headed to Mad Dog's house. When I got over there, I noticed he had a line of smokers at the front door. I shook my head and hopped out of the truck to see what the holdup was.

When I walked in, I saw exactly what the holdup was. They had done fucked around and let one overdose. I shook my head as I stepped over her body as she lay on the floor with foam coming out of her mouth.

"What's good Maddog?" I asked once I walked in the kitchen.

"Man, tryna let the bitch die so I can throw her out back." he said and I shook my head. I grabbed a knife out of the kitchen and walked back into the living room.

I moved Lucky out of my way and slit her throat from ear to ear. "Damn." Lucky said as he looked at me with wide eyes. Nigga was acting like he ain't never seen nobody get killed before.

"Get her out of here now." I stated as I stood upright.

I waited for Lucky and another guy who's name I couldn't recall at the moment, to grab her and carry her out of the room. I grabbed a towel out of the bathroom and wiped the blood up from the plastic that covered the living room floor and left.

    Before I went home, I made sure I stopped to grab Nichole a phone. I'm not sure what she likes so I settled on the Galaxy Core Prime and a pink case then headed to the house.

Nichole

It felt like I laid in the bed for hours and when I checked the time, I realized I had. I hadn't eaten a thing since this morning when Murda stopped to get us food and it's now almost 3 o'clock in the evening. I know I dozed off several times throughout the day, maybe that's why I didn't realize I was hungry again. Either that or I've been hungry so much that it's normal now.

I sat up slowly so I could look in the mirror but I was afraid of what I would see. "You got this girl." I said out loud to myself. It was my way of giving myself a confidence boost. I climbed out of bed and walked up to the dresser with my head down.

I looked up slowly and as soon as my eyes connected with my reflection, tears sprang from them and slid down my purple cheeks. The ice helped a little but I still looked like a monster. My face was almost back to its normal size and I'm sure the ice had plenty to do with that.

I grabbed the bag of water and walked back to the kitchen to refill it with ice. Once I was done, I made my way back to my room and sat on the bed. For some reason, I wanted to continue to read the letters, but I was afraid I would get pissed off all over again. Sad part about it is, I want to understand why he stayed away from me. I want to understand how he was able to watch his own child, his own flesh and blood go through what I went through. There were times my mom only had enough food for three and I was the only one who didn't eat. She would give me a cup filled with water and send me to my room while her, Nette and Sabrina ate. If anything, she should have been the one with a cup of water!

I got down on my knees on the floor next to the bed so I could grab the box when I heard footsteps coming towards me. My heart rate sped up as I turned around slowly.
"Girl what the hell you doing on the floor?" Murda asked with a frown on his face.
I just stared up at him as I took in his appearance. He had on fresh white air force ones, crisp black Levi jeans and a white tee shirt with blood splattered across the front.
"You did it again?" I asked with a slight frown.
It was more so because of disappointment than it was anger. For some reason when he grabbed me I felt safe, so I guess I was kind of hoping he would play it cool while I was living here but I guess not.

What if someone followed him here because he killed their family member? What if I was killed in retaliation to something that he did to someone else? I have to hurry up and get out of here because I don't want to become a victim to anything or anyone because of something I had nothing to do with.

"I bought you a phone." he said to me as he walked completely inside of my room.
I stared up at him from my position on the floor as he handed me the phone. A big bright smile spread across my face as I ripped it open. I heard him chuckle lightly and felt my panties get moist. I don't have time to be changing panties already, hell I only have three pair. The thought alone made me shake my head slightly.

"What's wrong?" he asked and I looked back up at him. I was too embarrassed to tell him so I just shook my head again. Murda stayed in the room with me and watched me activate the phone but he didn't say a word. It was fine though because his presence was a welcomed distraction.

Once I was done setting everything up, Murda grabbed the phone out of my hand.
"I'm putting my number in here, so if you need me call me. If I don't answer the phone just send me a text message." he said, walking away before I could respond to him.
I wonder why he's so cold towards me but at the same time loving. Well, not really loving but caring. Hell I don't know, I'm only 17. Everybody is loving compared to my family though so I'll take what I can get from Murda.
I quickly dialed Amber's number and saved it.
"Who is this?" she answered.
"Nichole." I answered as I stared down at my toes. I shook my head at how pitiful I looked and felt.
"Biiiiiitch! You got a phone huh?" Amber screamed in my ear.
She was so loud that I was able to sit the phone on the floor next to me and still hear her.
"Yes, I'm so excited." I said dryly.
"Are you being sarcastic right now hoe?!" Amber asked and I could only imagine the side eye that she would be giving me if we were in person.
"Naw, I'm serious." I answered because I actually was excited.

My only problem is, I was having a hard time showing it being as though my mind was really cloudy.

"Well you don't sound excited. What's wrong?" she asked with concern evident in her voice.

"My face looks worse. The swelling is down but it's all purple. Murda didn't help how I felt because he looked at me like I was a monster. Then on top of that my dad has been writing me letters every year for my birthday." I said all in one breath. It felt so good to be able to talk to someone. I knew without a shadow of doubt that I could trust Amber.

"Damn girl, do you wanna get out the house?" she asked. I thought about it for a moment but I didn't want to be seen like this. "I know what you're thinking but I can beat your face and you will look normal boo!" Amber screeched into the phone.

I sighed heavily because there is no way that she can make me look normal again.

Murda walked in and picked my phone up from the floor. He grabbed it so fast I didn't have time to snatch it away from him. He gave Amber directions to his house and told her he would be standing outside waiting for her to let her in. I sat on the floor with a confused look on my face as he handed me the phone back.

"Won't do no good sitting in the house." he stated then walked out of the door.

I had no idea how to feel about what had just happened so I just sat there with a dumb look on my face.

Around 4 o'clock, I heard Amber's mouth as he led her to my room. She walked in with a huge smile on her face and a large bag in her hand.

"Get up and sit on the bed." she said because I was still sitting on the floor.

As I stood up, I realized my leg had gone to sleep and it kind of hurt. Well it felt weird to put pressure on it. I wiggled my foot around in circles until I could feel it again then I moved my leg back and forth and climbed on the bed.

"You finished?" Amber asked with a smirk on her face. I nodded my head and smiled.

She sat her bag next to me so she could set everything up. There was so much makeup on my bed that I got a little scared about what she was about to do to me. By no means did I want to look like a clown. You how some chicks wear makeup and it's super cute, then you have the ones that don't know what color matches their skin tone so they look extra stupid. I don't want to look stupid.

"Close your eyes." Amber said. I felt myself frowning several times throughout the process because some of the makeup felt cold and wet. I just knew when I opened my eyes I would look like everybody's favorite clown.

It took a good thirty to forty-five minutes for her to finish my makeup. I don't know if that's how long it normally takes or if I was really fucked up and that's why it took so long.

"That beat on fleek!!!" she yelled as she jumped up and down. "Murda!" she screamed. "Mur-da!" she dragged out.

I heard a gun cock and Murda appeared in the doorway with his gun aimed directly at us. Amber jumped over the entire bed no lie! The bitch didn't even touch it on her way across it. It would have been funny as hell had this lunatic not had a gun still trained on me.

"Man what the hell you screaming." his voice trailed off once his eyes landed on me. He lowered the gun as he continued to stare at me with a blank expression on his face.

"Fuck I knew I shouldn't have let her do this." I said as I fought hard to keep the tears at bay.

Amber stood up slowly then walked around the bed once she realized he had lowered the gun.

"Bitch you cute, what you mad for?" she asked.

She followed my line of vision to Murda who was still just staring at me. She had a huge grin on her face as she looked between us, but I was completely lost. "How she look Murda?" she asked like he didn't just scare her across the bed. I shook my head as I dreaded his answer.

"Amazing." he said with a nonchalant attitude then left out of the room. "Don't yell like that no more." he said over his shoulder.

I climbed off the bed and kept my eyes closed until I bumped into the dresser. When I opened my eyes, my jaw hit the floor. There wasn't a bruise in sight baby! My eyes were a little red but nothing a bottle of clear eyes couldn't fix.

"Now we gotta get you dressed!" Amber said. I could tell she was excited but I really didn't have anything to choose from.

I settled on a pair of powder blue, high waist skinny jeans with a black crop top shirt. I said settled but I really in all honesty had nothing to choose from, so I guess it's not really settling.

"I don't have any shoes." I said as I looked at her. I watched Amber do a light jog out of my room.

"Stop fucking running through my shit!" Murda yelled and I shook my head.

When Amber came back, she tossed me a pair of those flip flops from the dollar general that only cost a dollar. They were black so they matched. "Let's go!" she said with a smile after I slipped the shoes on.

Amber

I hooked my girl up and I didn't miss the way Murda was looking at her either. I'm going to be sure I tell her that his extra crazy ass is feeling her! Looks like a love connection is happening.

Anyway, he gone make me slap his ass about his mouth though. Now about that gun, I almost shitted bricks! My flight or fight senses definitely kicked in. Wait, maybe I should call them spider senses since I hopped my ass on the other side of the room. I know that's something I'm going to laugh about later but baby, right now ain't the time. My fucking back is throbbing and everything from the beat on Nichole's face. Shawty bad! I keep a couple bad bitches with me! Ha! I damn near started twerking.

As Nichole and I were walking out of Murda's clean estate, he came out of nowhere. I thought it was so cute how stuck on stupid he was, yet again.
"Where y'all going?" he asked Nichole.
He was staring at her so hard that I knew he could see her soul! She turned around and looked at me but I just shrugged my shoulders. I didn't have a destination in mind, hell I never do. I usually just end up wherever I end up. Dating Ant sometimes is like dating my damn self, so I can't ever count on him to be available for me to lay under when I'm free. School normally takes up most of my day but since we are suspended all of next week, I don't know what we will be doing.

"Here." he said to her as he stuck his hand deep down in his pocket. She walked up to him slowly as he gave her a wad of money. "Go buy some shit. I know yeen got everything you need." he said without taking his eyes off of her.

I know he didn't because I was watching him like a hawk. I needed to make sure he wasn't gone pull another gun out or something.

"Ok. Thanks." she said as she looked down at the ground. I'm going to curse her ass out as soon as she gets in the car.

"Call me when you're on your way back so I can let you back in." he said to her.

She nodded her head but didn't look back at him. She's got to be the scariest person I've ever met! I smiled at him then turned around to hop in the car.

I watched Murda walk past us to his truck and pull off. I followed suit.

"So what y'all been doing?" I asked, because the way he looks at her I know they have done something!

"Nothing. He just got here right before I called you." she said, like living in Murda's fine ass house was nothing.

I swear she's my girl and I love her but she's so damn green! I don't even think she's fucking.

"Bitch you live with Murda and you acting like it ain't shit!" I said as I weaved through traffic. We were about to tear the mall up with that money baby!

"Well it's only been a couple of hours." she said then looked up at me.

I watched her pull her phone out and take a selfie. I laughed at her but focused my attention on the road. The last thing I needed to do was get in a wreck.

"C'mon." she said as she leaned over in my direction. I met her halfway and smiled for the camera. The picture turned out real cute but what else would you expect from us?

"I'm about to make a Facebook." she said as she thumbed through the app store on her phone.

I sank down in my seat because she just opened the door for me to tell her what happened. I have no idea how to tell her because I've never been good at stuff like this.

"Razor took a picture of you all beat the fuck up and sent it to Kisha. Kisha posted it on Facebook, and Bianca sent it to me. That's how I knew what happened to you. I called Ant so he could find Razor but they already had him and that's how I knew to come to the warehouse." I said all in one breath.

I figured since I didn't know how to sugar coat it that I would just give it to her straight with no chaser. When she hadn't responded, I glanced over at her and could see her ears were turning red. I knew she was heated because when I saw the picture I was heated too. She never responded to me. When we got to a stop light, I leaned over to see what she was doing and she was completing the Facebook setup.

I was beyond confused because I expected her to be pissed off and snapping or something. Anything other than what she was doing. I continued to drive and a few minutes later, we pulled up to the mall.

Wolfchase mall is by far the biggest mall in Memphis, and I planned to drag Nichole through every store they had for women. I climbed out the car and watched her take another selfie. The way she was turned, I was in it so I smiled. She uploaded the pictures as she walked around the car to get to me.

"What the hell you doing?" I asked because I was so confused.

"That pictured surfaced last night right?" she asked as we walked through the parking lot to get to the mall.

I nodded my head as I waited for her to explain.

"I'm taking these today with no bruises. I'm not even going to respond to those because these are now out there. I'll just deny any of it happened. Everybody that was in the cafeteria knows we won." she said then shrugged her shoulders.

I smiled at her as we walked inside the mall. This bitch bought so many pairs of panties I didn't know what to say to her. She got some cute dresses and even copped me a few too. By the time we left the mall it was going on 7 o'clock.

It was getting dark. It was the end of April and Nichole's birthday was coming up. I wondered what she planned on doing for it so I asked, but she just shrugged her shoulders like it was no big deal. I'm going to find something for us to get into.

"You ready to go home?" I asked and she shook her head. I wonder how it's going to be with her going from living with all women to living with a man. A man she hardly knows at that. Then on top of that, anyone with eyes can see how he was looking at her.

"Do you still have a crush on Murda?" I asked but my phone started ringing and interrupted our conversation. When I glanced down and saw it was Bianca, I rolled my eyes so hard I got dizzy. "What's up?" I answered with my car's Bluetooth.
"So y'all went to the mall without me huh?" Bianca asked. I could hear the jealousy in her voice as I shook my head. "Yeah, how you know?" I asked.
"Cause little Ms. Prissy posted it on Facebook and tagged y'all location!" she said with an attitude.
I started laughing because I have no idea what her damn problem is. It's like it came out of nowhere. "Anyway what y'all hoes fina do?" she asked and I shook my head at how bipolar she was acting.
"Hit up the movies." I answered.
"The one we use to go to?" she asked.
"Yep." I answered.
"Oh ok well have fun." she said then hung the phone up.

"So we're going to the movies?" Nichole asked with a smile on her face. I can tell she's not used to hanging out at all. It's Saturday night but we aren't old enough to get in a club. I have a fake ID but I know Nichole doesn't so a club is out of the question for us.

I checked my phone and realized my parents hadn't called me all day. Mind you, I left out in the middle of the night and haven't returned. I shook my head at how my parents don't care about me at all.

Nichole

I noticed the mood in the car shift almost as soon as it shifted. I glanced over at Amber and saw her shaking her head. I can trust her but I want her to know that she can trust me too.
"What's wrong?" I asked as I looked at her but she shook her head. I could tell something was wrong but I was not about to force her to tell me what it was.

Her phone started to ring again and I was going to say something if it was Bianca again. I've had almost enough of her backstabbing ass. She had one more time to say something about me behind my back that she wouldn't say to my face and I was going to beat her up!
I've already figured Bianca out. As a matter of fact, I figured her out a long time ago. She's all bark with no bite. That's why Amber ended up fighting all of her battles.

"Where you at ma?" her boyfriend Ant's voice came through the speakers.
"On my way to the movies." she answered him. I watched her smile return to her face at the sound of his voice.
I can't wait until I find a love of my own. One that won't leave me after I have his child like my dad did my mom.
"Who the hell you going to the movies with?!" he asked her. I could tell he had an attitude. It took

everything in me not to laugh at him. It was kind of cute.

"Nichole." she answered as she pulled in the parking lot of the movies.

"Oh ok. Call me after you drop her off." he said then hung up the phone.

"Him and Murda must be related." I said more so to myself but loud enough for Amber to hear me.

"Why you say that?" Amber asked as we both got out of the car.

I looked towards the movie theatre and saw that it was packed! I'm glad my face is beat to perfection! "Because Murda makes demands too but he walks away before you have time to say anything." I said as we made our way to the line.

"Look at you acting like you know a nigga." she said as she laughed at me. I laughed too because I did say that like we're longtime friends.

I mean I practically know him because I've been watching him for a few years now from my window. I had the biggest crush on him but now I'm not so sure. I think fear has replaced that feeling I had but at the same time, I don't think he would ever let anything happen to me. It's weird I guess.

"You need to let him know what's going on so he won't be somewhere waiting on you or worse." Amber said. She confused me with that one.

"What could be worse?" I asked with a frown on my face.

"He can forget you live there and get ghost." she said with a serious expression on her face. I stared at her with a blank expression on my face then my jaw dropped. Amber turned around to see what I was looking at and when she turned back around she shook her head.

"Don't worry about them hoes. We fina watch this movie and go home." Amber said.

She's normally a hot head so for her to say that to me was a shock. I expected her to walk up to them and start swinging again like she did in the cafeteria. I pulled my phone out so I could text Murda like Amber said.

"What you doing?" Amber asked. I rolled my eyes because she literally just told me to text him.

"Texting him." I said.

I didn't want to say his name because we were around a bunch of females and I didn't want to give anyone the impression that we were dating. Especially since we weren't.

Nichole: Hey, I'm at the movies w/ Amber. be home afterwards

Murda: What time da movie start???

"Can you see what time the scary movie starts over there?" I asked Amber as I pointed. Once she walked over to see, she came back to tell me.

Nichole: 720

Murda: b home by 930

I stood next to Amber with my mouth wide open as I read the last message over and over again. "What's wrong?" she asked once she realized what I was doing.

She grabbed the phone out of my hands and read our brief conversation. She started laughing but for the life of me I didn't know what was funny.
"I'll get you home by 9:15!" she said in between laughing. "Close ya mouth doll." she said with a smile. I shook my head and closed my mouth.

Everything went fine in the movies. It wasn't until I was headed back to Amber's car that a problem arose. "You like jumping people huh?" I heard a voice say from behind me. When I turned around, I saw that it was Kisha and her sister. I rolled my eyes because I was alone. I wasn't scared but come on now.... two against one, you do the math. I shouldn't have left Amber in the bathroom. She had to use it and I suggested that I go get the car and bring it up to the door. I only suggested that so I could drive her car, now I'm regretting it.
I quickly sent Amber a text message so I could let her know what was about to go down and sat my phone on top of the car. I turned around to face them and for the life of me I couldn't figure out what I had to do with my sister sleeping with Kisha's sister boyfriend. Hell I don't even know what Kisha's sister's name is so why are they coming at me and not Antionette. I shook my head as I stared at them.
"I thought you whooped her ass?" her sister asked her as she looked at me with a frown.
"I did see." Kisha replied and gave her the phone. I smiled on the inside because I knew she was showing her the picture Amber told me about.

"Bitch please you know you didn't win." I said with a smirk on my face.

They both glared at me then Kisha slid her phone down in her pocket. I knew they were about to jump me, I'm just glad I got some rest so I could hold up for myself. They may win, but one of them will have a well whooped ass. I stared at them as I weighed my options. I could tell they were talking but I couldn't tell you what was being said because I tuned them completely out as I watched them.

Kisha's sister is bigger than her so I'll take my chances fighting her straight up. Kisha is a bit taller than me but she can't fight that good, so I'll just focus on her sister. I took a step forward and swung in one motion.

"Shit Lisa." Kisha said to her sister.

Lisa stumbled backwards but she regrouped fast and came swinging at me in a windmill fashion. I side stepped and pushed her into Amber's car. I was completely in my zone like I had taken one of those pills that allows you to access 100% of your brain.

"Bitch!" Kisha screamed as she tackled me into Amber's car.

Luckily for me, I caught my balance and kicked her with the bottom of my foot since she tackled me from behind. Lisa was swinging at me again. I jumped behind Kisha and pushed her into Lisa and they both stumbled backwards.

I shook my head at the fact that I wasn't losing but I was fighting two people. Then they both came at me at the same time. I backpedaled in attempt to give myself time to figure out what to do but I tripped over a curb and fell on my ass.

"Oh shit they jumping!" I heard someone yell out. Lisa and Kisha began to kick me. One of them was kicking my stomach and the other one was kicking me in my back. I had no idea what to do but I was not about to give up. Especially not while people were watching. I'd had enough of people putting their hands on me.

    I grabbed Lisa's foot and twisted it. It caused her to fall to the ground a few steps away from me.

"Aargh! Fuck!" she said as she sat up slowly. Kisha's dumb ass ran to her sister's aid to help her up. While she was helping her, I sat up and noticed my hands were bleeding. I must have scuffed my hands when I fell over the curb.

As I stood up slowly my back burned like hell. I bent over in pain. "You bitch!" I heard Lisa say followed by a gun being cocked.

Amber

The movie was so freaking good but all the food I consumed during the movie had my stomach tore completely up. I normally don't use public bathrooms, but I honestly didn't think I would be able to hold it since I had to drop Nichole off and then head on home.

When I told Nichole that I couldn't hold it, she told me to go ahead and she would go get the car. I didn't even think to ask her if she knew how to drive. As a matter of fact, I didn't think about the fact that I gave her my keys until I had started to use the bathroom. I strolled through my Facebook news feed as I sat on the toilet seat that I had wrapped with tissue paper. My breath got caught in my throat when I read Kisha's latest Facebook update:

Kisha Dabaddest: Fina beat a bitch up yep!

I tried to rush mother nature so I could go help my friend. I was concentrating hard and I know this is too much information but fuck it, better out than in right? Anyway, when I got a message from Nichole telling me Kisha and her sister were about to jump her, I quickly stood up, cleaned myself off and ran out of the bathroom.

By the time I made it outside there was a huge crowd of people, so I knew what they were watching. I pushed through the crowd roughly until I made it halfway through. Someone pushed me down as I was trying to push my way through. I hit the ground hard! I looked up with anger in my eyes as I stared at my ex-boyfriend, Shun. He and I broke up strangely for this exact reason. He couldn't keep his hands to himself. My mouth is way to flip to date someone abusive. Man, that man had to slap me upside my head damn near every day. I tried leaving him on several occasions but he would always still show up like nothing had happened. Mind you I was only 12 years old, he was 17 and I was just happy that a guy had showed interest in me.

By the age of 11, I wasn't round anymore, my body had started to form a shape. So by 12, I had more titties and ass then everyone in my grade; and they still made me feel fat because they were all so skinny. Shoot I'm really just now realizing that I'm not fat, I just have more to love. I have the big booty and big breasts but I also have a big stomach but my man loves it all.

"Watch where you going!" Shun snapped as he looked down at me with pure disgust.
I matched his look as I got off the ground. I stood up straight and dust my pants off and pushed him right back. He stumbled back into a lady and she shoved him back in my direction. I watched him reel back and I knew he was about to knock me out. I instantly regretted shoving him back. A random guy jumped in front of me and pushed Shun backwards.
"Man what the fuck? That's a female!" the man spat angrily.
"Fuck her! She came through here and pushed me!" Shun snapped but I noticed he didn't even try to hit the guy back.
"Weak bitch." I thought to myself as I stood up and watched the brief interchange between the two.

The random guy raised his shirt up slightly and I only knew he showed him a gun because Shun's eyes got big and he took a step back.

"You got it." Shun said as he took another timid step backwards with his hands in the air. "I'll catch you later." Shun said to me and my heart sunk down in my stomach.

"You good?" the guy turned around and asked me.

"Yes thanks." I answered him.

"I'm Jonathan." he said with his hand extended.

"Amber." I said as I shook his hand.

POW! The sound of a gun being shot brought me back to the reason why I was pushing the crowd in the first place.

"Nichole!" I screamed as I ran passed Jonathan and pushed through the rest of the crowd. It proved to be harder to do after the sound of gunfire because everybody started to scatter. "Nooooo!" I screamed out when I saw a body sprawled out on the ground. Tears clouded my vision as I made my way through the rest of the people who were seemingly running for their lives.

Murda

I decided to go hang out in the hood with Boobie while I waited for Nichole to finish her movie. I didn't mind her going anywhere until I saw her with makeup on. She looked so damn beautiful that I gave her little young ass a curfew. I need to find out if she's legal or not so I know if I need to pursue her or not. She caught my attention on some love at first sight shit the day I knocked her over but after Amber hooked her up, all I wanted was to keep her trapped away in the house.

I shook my head to get her image out of my mind as I pulled up on the block. I parked a few houses down then walked the rest of the way to Boobie's trap. I know Boobie closes up shop around 8 and everybody pretty much parties after that with no smokers allowed. He's the only person I allow to do that because he makes the same amount of money in the hours that he's open as the other trap houses that are open 24 hours a day. I have no idea how he does it and I really don't care because he's making me money and still gets to enjoy his life.

"What's up Murda?" Boobie greeted as he stood up to give me dap.

"Hey Darnell." Tawanna sang in that annoying high pitched voice that I hated all the way through school.

I've known Tawanna since the sandbox days. We use to live right next door to each other for about four years. Her mom and my mom were real tight way back, before her mom started doing drugs. Shit pissed me off so bad when her mom asked me for some hard. I just shook my head and walked away.

I'm all about my money but I don't deal with hard. My pops has been trying to get me to extend my brand for the last two years but I'm not selling anything that does what hard does to my people. I got every type of weed you can name though and that's how I'm making so much money. I got this new shit called deaf. They say when you hit it, you don't hear shit for a good five minutes or so. I have to get with Animal so he can send someone out to California to get it from my boy Martez.

"We ain't speaking?" Tawanna asked. I nodded my head in her direction to acknowledge her so she would quit talking to me. I don't know why she drags her words when she talks now, it makes her already annoying voice more annoying.
"Oooh shit! You know her?" Stephanie asked Tawanna as she handed her her iPhone. I shook my head at how simple minded broads are always somewhere gossiping. Neither one of them have a pot to piss in or a window to throw it out of yet they are always talking about somebody else.

I leaned against the house next to where Boobie sat and watched the crowd for a few minutes. It was crazy how niggas were drawn to the street life to get hoes and these hoes were drawn to it to get a nigga. People don't even realize that in most cases, the person you're meant to be with won't be in those place.

"Aye where Animal?" Boobie asked.
I shrugged my shoulders because my eyes caught a suspicious looking vehicle. It was an all-black box

Chevy and it was cruising through the neighborhood.

"Who is that?" I asked Boobie without taking my eyes off the car.

"I don't know." Boobie answered as he stood to his feet.

They continued their slow creep until they passed us and drove at a normal speed.

"Have they ever been through here before?" I asked Boobie.

"Naw." he said as he leaned over to get a look at the phone. "Damn somebody fucked her up!" Boobie exclaimed as he snatched the phone and handed it to me. When I looked at the picture of Nichole I wanted to break the phone in half.

"How you get this picture?" I asked Stephanie.

"Um.. I um…" she stuttered as she looked around for assistance. She shouldn't have brought her messy ass over here with the bullshit if she couldn't answer no questions.

"Who sent it?" I asked. I knew the look I was giving her is what was scaring her but I needed to know.

"Lisa. She said her little sister did this to her at school." she said as she looked away from me. Everybody grew silent as they waited for my next move.

I stuck my hand down in my pocket and pulled out a one-hundred-dollar bill. "Is that all?" I asked as I watched her eyes light up.

"They at the movies now fina fight her again." she rambled out. I stuck the money back in my pocket and Boobie fell out laughing.

"Man, you hell." he said as I dapped him up so I could go.

"Loose lips sink ships." I replied as I walked back to my truck. Just as I got to it, that all black Chevy was cruising through again. I watched them do the exact same thing they had done before.

After they passed, I looked over at Boobie to make sure he saw what I saw. He gave me a head nod so I knew he did. I hopped in my truck and sped off into the night to stop them bitches from jumping on Nichole again.

    When I pulled up in the parking lot, I knew where to go by the crowd that was forming. I parked and jumped out the truck as fast as I could. Nichole is a part of me now so if you disrespect her, then you're disrespecting me.

    I walked up behind Nichole just as the little bitches were about to attack her again. I pulled my gun from my waistband and cocked it in one swift motion. It froze them hoes in their tracks. I wasn't going to shoot them because it was a crowd of people and I had no way of knowing if they would tell or not. I also couldn't kill everybody here even if I wanted to.

    They stared at each other for a couple of minutes. I could tell Nichole was pissed off because of how hard she was breathing.

"He won't always be around." one of the other girls said.

Nichole turned around and looked in my eyes and I saw an all too familiar look. Murderous intent.

Nichole

I was beyond tired of the pure fuckery that life was constantly sending my way. What could I have possibly done to deserve the life I've been forced to live? Why am I constantly fighting battles for nothing? I'm always on the receiving end of the bullshit. For once in my life, I'd like to be the deliverer.
There's no more Ms. Nice Nichole. I'm Nicki in full effect right here, right now, at this moment in time. I want nothing more than to overcome being a victim and become the victor. When Murda cocked his gun, all it took was for Lisa to threaten me one more time to send me over the top.

I turned around and looked at Murda and for the first time since I've been watching him, I saw him. I knew and understood exactly why he does what he's known for. In our brief connection, in this moment, I totally get it.
In one swift motion I pulled the gun out his hand. I planted my feet and aimed the gun at Lisa. No one is going to hurt me ever again. I pulled the trigger. POW! I watched in slow motion as Lisa's body hit the ground and Kisha ran to her aid once again.

I felt my body being lifted off the ground as I was carried away from the scene of the crime. It was like I was having an outer body experience but I want to experience that feeling again. I'd never felt so alive in my life than I did behind the gun.

They say a person feels more alive right before they die but I think it's heightened right before you take a life. I found a new joy, a new love. Something that made me genuinely happy. My only regret is not being able to watch her die.

"Why the fuck did you do that?" Murda yelled as he slammed my body into the passenger seat of his truck roughly.

I didn't respond. My focus was on the crowd forming again slowly. I heard Amber scream out and it jerked me back to reality. I had just shot someone. I had just taken a life. I'm only 17 years old and I will spend the rest of my life behind bars.

"I need to fix this." I said as I hopped out of the truck before Murda had a chance to object.

I took off full speed until I was back in front Lisa, Kisha and now Amber.

"There she go. Somebody call the police." I heard someone yell.

"Bitch I thought you got shot!" Amber screamed with a tear stained face.

She ran directly into me, almost knocking me over in the process as she hugged me tight.

"Is she..." I let my voice trailed off but I know she knew what I was asking.

"Naw you shot her though so we gotta go!" she said and pulled my arm towards her car.

When we made it to her car, Murda stopped his truck directly behind us. I looked at him as he stared at me and shook his head.

"Take your ass straight home!" he snapped then pulled in the spot next to us.

I watched him climb out of his truck as we backed out of the parking spot. He grabbed Lisa and threw her body in the backseat of his truck.

"Go now!" he yelled at us as he turned around and forced Kisha inside his truck as well.

Murda

I couldn't believe Nichole had it in her to shoot any damn body. I guess when you're constantly faced with bull shit, it eventually changes you. Well I know that it for sure changes you. I'm a walking testimony that life will do a number on you and leave you fucked up if you let it. The difference is, I never let it.

Nichole is hard headed as fuck though, because me slamming her down in my truck was my way of getting her out of dodge. Nooo, as soon as she heard Amber, she hopped out and ran to her. That shit wasn't necessary. How can you commit a crime like attempted murder then go back to the scene? That was by far the dumbest shit she had ever done. Yet and still, I tried to help her by grabbing Lisa and Kisha. My plan was to pay them to keep quiet so Nichole wouldn't get locked up. The police had a good twenty witnesses to the crime whom I'm sure would have testified but without a victim they couldn't do shit.

Here's where the problem comes in at. I told her to take her ass straight to the house and I would meet her there. I called up Animal and Juice and had them meet me at the warehouse so we could talk to these broads.

I pulled up to the warehouse before the guys because Animal had to go pick Juice up. They got there about ten minutes later and Animal unlocked the door.

"Please don't kill us." Lisa pleaded as she held on to her gunshot wound.

I examined the wound carefully and took note that Nichole is a pretty good shot. Not to mention I think that was her first time ever shooting. If it wasn't for the recoil on the gun causing it to kick back, Lisa would probably be dead or almost there. Lucky for her the bullet went through and through.

I grabbed her arm and lead her into the warehouse.

"What's going on?" Juice asked with a confused expression on his face.

I'm sure he has never seen women being brought here to be killed or threatened but there's a first time for everything. You never know what you may walk in on here. The warehouse is kind of one of those "anybody can die here" places. I'm not even sure if there are others places like this one in the world.

Anyway, I lead them into the same room we killed Rocket, Ruff and Razor in and made them take a seat in the chairs that still had their blood on it. Animal must have thrown the broken chair out because the fragments from the wood weren't there anymore. I could tell they started cleaning but something must have distracted them.

"So tell me what's the beef about." I demanded as I sat my gun on the table.

Lisa's eyes grew wide as she stared between the gun and I. I'm sure she thought we were about to do some triflin shit to them then kill them, but in all honesty, too many people saw me pull off with them for me to do anything and get away with it.

"Yall can't hear? Or you can hear but can't talk?" I asked as I laid my dentist belt across the table. I wasn't going to touch them at all but it was nothing for me to imply that they were going to die.

"We ain't got no beef with her." Kisha answered with a shaky voice.

That answer caught me off guard. Why would you jump someone at school then turn around and go where they are to jump them again if you have no beef with them?

"Explain why y'all fought at school." I said as I folded my hands across my chest.

"Her fat friend started that shit!" Kisha said as she rolled her eyes.

I heard Animal suck his teeth. When I glance in his direction, I could see his hand inching towards his piece on his waist.

"I know ain't nobody started shit for nothing. What did you do?" I asked as I grabbed a knife from the wall. I began to twirl it around my finger as I looked at her with an intense gaze. "Let's play truth or die." I suggested then turned around and smiled at the guys.

Juice had a worried look on his face but Animal knew that if I was going to kill them, I wouldn't have brought them here. Juice doesn't have that much common sense to put that together mentally but I'm going to teach him.

"W-w-what's that?" Kisha asked as her bottom lip trembled.

"It's like truth or dare. The rules are a bit different though." I said then paused to let it sink in. "I'm going to ask you a question. You're going to tell the truth. If for some reason you decide to lie, I will stab you. Each lie will get a stab until you die. Now

if you tell the truth, you will win the game." I explained.
The looks on their faces let me know that I had broken it down so good that it will forever be broken!
I smiled as I stood directly in front of Kisha. She was so scared that I could damn near smell it.
"Now, what did you do to start the fight at school?" I asked with a sinister look on my face.
"I was just staring at her and her friend came over snapping and hit me." she said.
I believed her because it was rushed out in a hurried pace. She had no time to think of a lie that time. I turned around and looked at Animal because he knows Amber better than anyone here.
"What do you think?" I asked him.
"Sounds like her." he stated plainly. I nodded my head.
"Why were you staring?" I asked as I thought about the kind of friend Amber appears to be.
I can tell she will have her back but she may be the reason she needs help.
"Nichole sister was messing with my sister's boyfriend." she said to me. She was now crying but those tears were doing nothing to me.
"So beef by association." I said as I nodded my head. "One of the quickest ways to get killed." I said as an FYI. I don't really understand how you can inherit someone else's beef. "Why did you go to the movies to fight her?" I asked just out of curiosity.
"Just… just.. just because." she answered somberly. I could tell she regretted it now but I need her to know not to do it again.

"I'm going to let you live but under one condition." I said and they both perked up. "Do NOT and I repeat DO NOT contact the police. If the police are contacted and it's out of your control, lie. If Nichole goes down for this, I'm going to come back and kill you." I said. I watched them shake their heads as they thanked me.

Juice blindfolded them for me and dropped them off at a gas station about ten miles out so they could call their ride. Animal and I waited outside for his return so we could lock the warehouse up.
"So what happened?" Animal asked as I wiped my back seats down in the truck.
I gave him a brief run through of what happened and he said he couldn't believe Nichole had it in her either. I had to agree that it was some shit straight out of a movie though.

When Juice came back, I dapped them up and went home. When I got there, my blood started to boil immediately. Nichole wasn't here. I'm not sure if they came and left or never came at all like they were supposed to. I left and drove to her mom's house because I thought she may have gone there since I said go home, but she wasn't there either. Her hoe ass sister, Antionette was more into me than she was about her sister. I shook my head but I didn't forget that I owed her and her mama one for what they did to her.

As I walked back to my truck it dawned on me that she has a phone now. I called her three times but it rang to voicemail each time. I began to worry and I didn't have Amber's number so I called Animal.

"What's up?" he answered.

"Man call ya girl and see where they at. They were supposed to be at my house but Nichole not answering.

"Iight bet." he said then hung his phone up.

I was not ready for the news he gave me when he called back. Fuck!

Amber

As soon as we pulled out the parking lot my phone started ringing. I was so hyped up off of my extra crazy ass friend that just went on beast mode and tried to merk a bitch, that I answered the phone without looking to see who it was.

"Yo!" I yelled out then glanced over at Nichole.

She wasn't saying anything but she looked like she was ok.

"Girl I heard Nichole just beat the dog shit out Kisha and her sister girl!" Bianca yelled through my car speakers. I smiled and glanced over at Nichole and she smiled back.

"Word travels fast." Nichole mumbled.

"She doesn't have a clue how big of a part social media plays in that." I thought to myself. "Yeah she did!" I said with a smile even though I didn't see the fight at all. I didn't even see a part of it.

"Bitch where were you?" Bianca asked.

"In the damn bathroom!" I said with a laugh as I shook my head.

Things wouldn't have turned out how they turned out had I been with her and I can guarantee you that one. We would've stomped a mud hole in them bitches so she wouldn't have had to shoot anyone.

"Where y'all heading? I got my grandma car and I'm trying to link up with my besties!" Bianca exclaimed. I could tell she was super excited.

"Meet us at the Waffle House. The one by the movies." I said after Nichole gave me the ok.

"Alright, so is it true though? Did Nicki try to kill a bitch?" Bianca asked but Nichole shook her head.

"See ya there chica!" I yelled then hung up the phone.

"Bitch I'm hungry for real." I said to Nichole and she laughed.

"Me too." she replied, so we headed to the Waffle House.

I could tell she needed that release she got because she was way more down to earth than she normally is.

We sat down at a table at the back of the restaurant and ordered our food. We both ordered All Star meals even though I'm sure we won't be able to finish it. As soon as Murda gets to his house and we not there, he's going to be blowing her phone up to get her ass there. Hell, he probably won't let her back out until all this shit dies down.

As we ate our food we were interrupted by the MPD.

"Are you Nichole Jackson?" he asked Nichole after he rudely pushed her plate across the table and knocked my plate in my lap. The grits were still hot so I jumped up out of the booth that I was sitting in.

"Fuck!" I screamed out as I glared at the police officer.

He reached for his baton. Instinctively I got on guard. If he thought I was going to stand here and let him beat me, he had another thing coming. He must not know who my parents are. They will bury the entire police department in a New York second.

"Ma'am keep your hands where I can see them." the officer said firmly to me.

"Yeah, you too." I replied as I eyed him carefully. Three more officers walked into the waffle house at the exact same time my phone started ringing. I glanced over at it and saw it was Ant but he would have to wait.

"Are you Nichole Jackson?" he asked her again. She still hadn't responded or even stopped eating. I think she knew what time it was so she was chilling like a real nigga. After she finished her bacon, she nodded her head to answer his question.

"Stand up for me and put your hands behind your back." he ordered.

"For fucking what?" I screamed out even though I already knew why they were here to arrest her.

My phone started ringing again and I saw it was Ant. Something must be wrong because he never calls me back to back. He normally gives me a chance to call him back or at least send a text message.

"Yeah?" I answered my phone just as the officer snatched Nichole out of the booth.

"Where y'all at?" Ant asked but I was distracted by how the officer was handling my girl.

"Yeen gotta be so rough with her! What you arresting her for?" I screamed out as I followed closely behind them.

One of the other officers stopped me from getting out the door.

"I know my rights mu'fucker, you can't stop me from going outside." I said to the officer.

"What's going on?" Ant yelled in my ear.

"I'll arrest you for obstruction of justice." the officer said with an attitude. I always hate female officers because they are so much more aggressive like they got a point to prove or something.

"Obstruct these nuts!" I snapped as I pushed passed her. "Nichole don't say nothing! I'm going to send you a lawyer!" I screamed out to her.

Ant was steady screaming in my ear but I needed to make sure my girl was ok. I watched her until she nodded her head and I walked back in the store.

I paid for our food then grabbed our things.

"Amber!" Ant yelled in my ear.

"What shit?" I snapped because he was getting on my damn nerves screaming in my ear like I didn't have shit going on over here.

"Who the fuck you talking to?!" he snapped and I could only imagine the vein in the middle of his forehead protruding at this very moment.

I sighed dramatically as I rolled my eyes and hopped in my car. I needed to go home and get my parents to help get Nichole out because God knows her mama wasn't going to do shit.

"Did Nichole just get arrested?" he asked after he managed to calm himself down.

"Yes." I said as I tried hard not to hang the phone up on him.

"Iight bet." he said and hung the phone up. I hate when he does that shit like I'm one of his boys.

"Ugh!" I said out loud as I threw my phone out of frustrations.

As soon as I pulled off my phone started ringing. When I looked at the phone blinking on the floor I saw it was Bianca. I rolled my eyes and continued to drive home. Now is not the time for gossip and I know she's just going to piss me off.

I drove straight home and ran several traffic lights on my way there. As soon as I pulled in the driveway my mom was getting out of her BMW.

She looked at me and rolled her eyes before she walked away to the door. Now a normal parent would have saw their daughter distraught and ran to her but of course mine don't care. I'm not going to get into their lack of parenting skills at the moment though.

"Mom my best friend got arrested and I need you or dad to represent her." I said as I followed her inside of the house.

"So you decided to come home huh?" my mom asked. She completely ignored my plea for Nichole.

"Mom listen. She's only 17 and her mom doesn't care about her. Can you please, please, please help her?" I pleaded once again.

My mom turned around with her nose in the air as she looked at me.

"Maybe you shouldn't have such ghetto friends." she stated plainly as she walked passed me. I could feel the tears building as I tried to keep them at bay.

"If she was able to pay you, will you help her?" I asked because I was relentless in my pursuit to help Nichole. My mom was the best criminal defense attorney in Memphis. The only person that could get you off besides her is my dad.

"Yes." she said.

"Ok. How much is your fee?" I asked. I didn't care what price she said because my man getting money and he will do whatever he can to make sure I'm happy.

"$1500 to look at the case." she answered in an uppity tone.

"Bitch is that it?" is what I wanted to say but I nodded my head and walked back out of the door.

Murda

BAM! I punched a hole in the wall after I hung up with Animal. I told that damn girl to bring her ass straight here and what the fuck do she do? Go to the fucking waffle house! Who does stupid shit like that? How you gone shoot a bitch in front of twenty mu'fuckers and then go eat at the waffle house? That has gots to be the dumbest shit I've heard in a long time.

She lucky I got a lawyer on hold. I got the best lawyer in Memphis on lock because I keep her ass on retainer. I don't really like the bitch but she's the best. I grabbed my phone and called her.
"Thompson's and Associates." she answered. I shook my head at the sound of her voice.
"Aye I need you to meet me in county." I said to her as I grabbed my keys and ran out of the door.
"Pertaining to?" she asked.
"Ion talk on phones. You're already paid. Be there before me." I said then hung the phone up.
She lives closer to the precinct than I do, so she better get there before me.
We pulled up at the same time, so I must have caught her at a bad time. I told her everything about Nichole that she needed to know and sent her on her way. I waited in the lobby as she went back to talk to sergeant and the arresting officer along with the detectives. When she walked back out she had a smile on her face.

"What's up?" I asked as I stood to my feet.

"I got good news and bad news." she started but stopped like she was waiting on me to tell her something.

I walked out of the police station and she followed me.

"The bad news is, it's Saturday so she has to stay in lock up until Monday then she can see the judge. Also she admitted to fighting someone. I don't know what else happened but they are saying she shot someone. They don't have any evidence since they don't have a cooperating victim. She should be out Monday." she explained.

"Cool, cool. I'll see you in court." I said as I made my way to my truck.

"9 o'clock sharp." she yelled at my back.

"This is going to be a long weekend." I thought to myself as I made my way home. I hit Animal up to let him know I got a lawyer for Nichole so Amber wouldn't worry about her.

I was up and dressed by 8, then made my way down to the courthouse. I wasn't the only one early because Amber was already there. She was sitting directly behind Ms. Thompson. I could see her burning holes in the back of her head. I wonder what they're problem is with one another.

She told me 9 but it looked like they were going to get started early. I guess looks could be deceiving because we didn't have to rise for the judge until 9 on the dot.

They brought Nichole out first and she wouldn't look up. It wasn't until I caught a glimpse of the side of her face that I knew why. She's was feeling insecure again since they more than likely made her shower. Her bruises were in clear view. I watched her helplessly with shackles around her ankles and wrists that connected in the middle. "What happened to your face Ms. Jackson?" the judge asked.

"I fell your honor." she replied.

I couldn't believe she gave him the same dumb answer she gave me. I shook my head as I stared at her.

"You fell huh? Is it possible that that happened while you were fighting at the movie theatre?" he asked. She didn't respond. "Ok. Let's see here." the judge said as he shuffled through paperwork. he was probably trying to find her case file.

"Your honor, I've filed for a dismissal of this case with prejudice." Ms. Thompson stood up and said. The judge frowned at her as he peered at her over his glasses.

"This is an attempted murder charge. On what grounds is there cause for dismissal?" the judge inquired.

"Your honor there is no victim in this case. There entire case is based solely on the words of someone over the phone." she explained.

"Is that right?" he asked the state's lawyer.

"Your honor we do have a witness to the crime." he said with a shaky voice.

"Let's see them." the judge said.

"Your honor she will like for us to play her recorded witness statement." he said as he stood to his feet.

"Your honor I haven't had time to view this piece of evidence. They withheld it to blindside me." Ms. Thompson stood to her feet and shouted. I could tell she didn't like not getting her way but I'm glad she's on Nichole's side.

"I'm presenting it now your honor. I thought she would be able to make it in but she wasn't." the other lawyer stated.

"Your honor you have to strike this from evidence." Ms. Thompson demanded.

The judge frowned at her. "I'll allow it." he said.

"I saw them fight at school then at the movies. I don't know where Nichole got her gun from but she pulled it out and shot Lisa." I heard a female voice say on the recorder.

"That bitch!" Nichole yelled as she stood up! Amber jumped up and stormed out of the courtroom. "She's lying!" Nichole yelled. Ms. Thompson was trying to calm her down but she wasn't listening.

"Order! Order! Order in the court!" the judge yelled out.

Nichole continued to shout obscenities out. "Ms. Thompson control your client! One more outburst and she will get thirty days' contempt!" The judge shouted but Nichole continued to cry out. I was so mad that I couldn't help her as I sat back and watched.

"Get her outta here!" The judge demanded. I shook my head and left out of the building.

I waited outside for Ms. Thompson. "Who's the witness?" I asked. She gave me a quizzical look.

"I can't give you that information." she answered. I shook my head at her. She knew without a shadow of a doubt that I would make their witness disappear.

"That recording alone is not enough to take her down. She will get a chance to face her accuser at the trial." she said then walked off in a hurried fashion.

As I headed to my car I felt my phone vibrate in my pocket. I pulled it out and it was a text message from an unknown number.

unknown: that was Bianca James

Nichole

"Nichole!" I heard someone scream my name. I opened my eyes slowly because I was hoping I wasn't in the same place that I had been when I fell asleep.
"Girl you gotta quit screaming in your sleep like that." Shirley said to me.
I could see the anger written all over her face. She was tired of helping me fight everyday but I wasn't tired of fighting. Not to mention I couldn't control the nightmares I kept having of the night I shot Lisa's stupid ass. Murda did everything he could to help me that night but I didn't listen. One thing for sure though, I learned to keep my grass cut low.

    I remembered all of the warnings Shirley gave me when I first got here, but I'm a new person these days. I'm not the scary Nichole that got her ass handed to her about four times within 24 hours. Well that was thirty days ago and I go to court again in the morning.
    As I laid on my bunk, I stared up at the grey ceiling. I hated sleeping on the top bunk but Shirley got the bottom one. She was here first, so it ain't like I had a choice.
    It was bad enough I had to smell her feet everyday but I also had to smell it every time she used the bathroom. Man I smelled Shirley's funky ass every time she shifted her body. Every part of her smelled like something else. I'll never understand how you can still smell as bad as she does when you're forced to take a shower every day.

I've been working out heavily since I been here too so I'm looking real good. Everything's tight and right and when I get out of here, I'm going back to school to shit on them bitches.

Murda and I have talked on the phone every night since I been here and he comes to see me every Sunday. We even write letters back and forth. We've gotten extremely close over this month and I can't wait to get out so we can solidify our union.

I've grown to love everything about him and the way he's held me down. I know he's still been out there wreaking havoc on mu'fuckers and stacking his paper but I made sure I told him to leave Nette, my mama and especially Bianca for me. Amber got mad because I didn't want her to do anything until I got out. I told them both to act like everything was fine but when I come home, they will feel me long before they see me.

I swung my legs over the bed as I sat up and waited for them to unlock the cell door so I could go eat breakfast. It was eerily quiet this morning but it be like that sometimes. When I heard the sound of the cell's door unlock, I hopped out of bed and made my way to the cafeteria.

"What's up Nik?" Monica asked as I passed her cell. I threw my hand up at her and kept it right on moving.

She sped walk to catch up to me as she made small talk about her cellmate eating her pussy the night before. I could care less about what they had going on in their cell.

I had about three different bitches on three separate occasions try me. I fought all of them too and I couldn't believe I won. Shit, I was so pumped after I won three jail fights that I transformed into Amber. Not necessarily Amber, but you know her aggressive personality. It was like I was walking around with a little Amber sitting on my shoulder and she would tell me when I needed to punch a bitch in the mouth.

After two weeks, I hardly had any problems. I always walked around like I had a chip on my shoulder. Maybe more so a point to prove because I actually did. I needed these bitches to know I wasn't the Nichole I was when I got here. The Nichole I am now doesn't take shit off nobody. I know that since I survived these thirty days with criminals, that I can definitely survive in these streets.

"Do you hear me talking to you?" Monica asked.
I had completely tuned her out. I didn't even realize she was still talking to me. I was lost in my thoughts as we walked into the cafeteria. A few people looked at me and looked away and some just stared. I didn't mind either way though.

I grabbed my tray and sat at a nearby empty table. I began to eat the fruit off my tray with leg propped up when there was a tray slammed down in front of me. When I looked up, I came eye to eye with Big Tiffany.

Since I'd been here, I'd heard a whole lot of shit about her but I had never had an encounter with her. It would be just my luck that the day before my court date, the day I would hopefully become free, I have a run in with her extra big ass. I hope like hell she don't want to fight because I was trying to go

home with a cute face not bruised the fuck up like I was when I got here.
"Why you be doing all that screaming and shit?!" Big Tiffany asked. I shrugged my shoulders and continued to eat the fruit off of my tray. "You ignoring me?" she asked.
I didn't respond to that dumb ass question because it was clear that I wasn't ignoring her.

As I reached for another slice of banana, she swiped my tray off the table. I heard a few aah's from other inmates once my tray collided with the floor. I shook my head as I stood to my feet and headed out the door.
Before I got to the door, I noticed three girls walk in front of it. I glanced around and for the first time, there was no guards posted anywhere in the cafeteria. I shook my head, took a deep breath and turned around slowly. I had no idea what to do. I knew I would fight 'till death of me but I wasn't ready to die. Big Tiffany had everybody on payroll and I didn't have a bankroll to put anybody on payroll.

I looked around the cafeteria and all eyes were on us. I swallowed my fear as I stared at the big beast of a woman before me. *"Punch that bitch."* little Amber said from my shoulder. I wanted to listen like I'd done every other time something told me to fight, but this time it didn't seem like the smart thing to do.
"You interrupted my groove." Big Tiffany said as she took a step towards me.

"Let her make it baby." Monica said as she rushed to her side. Monica grabbed Big Tiffany's arm in an attempt to calm her down.

Big Tiffany snatched away and back handed her so hard that she hit the floor and slid away. "Daaammmmn!" I heard someone say while others laughed. Without a guard here to break up the fight before I died, I didn't know what to do.

I looked to my right and saw a white girl eating her breakfast with a fork like nothing was going on three steps away from her. I looked at her closely and could see what I thought was a shank sticking out the back of her shirt. *"If I could just get to that shank I'll be ok."* I thought to myself. Big Tiffany charged at me and I ran towards the white girl. She was completely oblivious to what was going on around her. Well at least that's what I thought. I had no idea she was a part of Big Tiffany's team until she turned around with a smile on her face. She stood up and pulled the shank out then jammed it into my stomach. I looked into her eyes with a questioning gaze as I dropped down to my knees.

She let the shank go as I stared at it. My hands began to tremble tremendously as I began to choke on my own blood. I tried to yank the shank out but I felt myself grow weak. I looked up at the white girl but she had sat back down just as quickly as she stood up and continued eating her meal. I heard loud commotion at the cafeteria's door and when I looked in that direction, I saw a swarm of guards flooding the cafeteria. My vision began to get blurry as I fell over on my side. I tried to fight it but I couldn't. I felt my eyes rolling until everything went black.

Sneak Peak

A Crazy Ghetto Love Story 3: Revenge is Best Served Cold

Linette king

Prologue

Frankie

I threw on one of my black jogging suits. I pulled my hood over my head as I did my best to sneak out of the house. I peeked in the room Alexis shares with Phat and saw she was knocked out. I guess that baby has been kicking her and Phat's ass, since they sleep a lot more now. As I passed Chris' room, I peeked in and noticed he was still gone. I let out a deep breath once I made it to the living room. *"Everybody's gone."* I thought to myself. I walked in the kitchen and grabbed my car keys and headed out the door.

As I walked to my car, I looked around to make sure nobody was watching me or about to pull up. I pulled off and headed to The Gadget Shop. I bought three tracking devices, headed back to the car and drove back home. Once I was home, I ran quickly in the house and got Vanessa's notebook to write her a letter. Once I was done, I activated two of the tracking devices. I put both remotes on her nightstand and labeled them both. I slid one of them in my pocket and carried the other one back out with me to the car along with some supplies I may need later.

I pulled out the yard and parallel parked and shut the engine off. About an hour or so later, one of Boss Lady's black vans pulled in. I waited patiently for them to enter our house like they always do, but they didn't go in. "Fuck!" I cursed under my breath. I made sure the overhead light was off so when I opened the car door to get out, it wouldn't come on. I slid out of the car slowly without closing the door behind me.

I stayed low to the ground as I crab walked to the van. I slid my body underneath the van and taped the tracking device to a pipe under it. I made sure it was on and crab walked back to my car. I slid in without being detected. The first part of my mission was complete.

I waited patiently for Vanessa, Chris and Phat to pull up and when they did, I began to wish I had some kind of way to give them a signal. The letter should be enough but I know they're going to be worried until they find the letter. Out of the corner of my eye I could see someone creeping along the side of the house heading towards the back. I wanted to let them know what I saw, but my cell phone was inside and I couldn't say anything without Boss lady's men knowing I'm alive.
"Being dead sucks!" I said out loud as I watched the person creep off until they were out of view.
I'm not a fighter like Vanessa so I would only cause more problems if I chase whoever that is down.

I waited until the transaction with the money was complete before I crank my car up. I watched them back out of the parking spot and pull away. I followed them with my lights off until we got on the highway, then I turned my lights on. It took them about an hour to turn off onto a rocky road and I continued going straight. I made a U-turn and when I got to that road, I cut my lights off and drove slowly. I drove for about 30 minutes before I saw what looked like an iron gate. I began to grin from ear to ear because we were finally one step ahead of this bitch.

  I parked my car but left the engine running as I hopped out and did a light jog through the trees up to the gate. I saw guards everywhere and it made the smile wipe off my face instantly.
"Fuck, how do I get in?" I said out loud to myself.
"You don't." a familiar voice said from behind me.
I turned around slowly and came face to face with the person that started this horrible chain of events.
"Are you working with her?" I asked as I took a cautious step back.
He held his hands up as he took a step towards me as he shook his head. "Why are you doing this?" I asked as I looked past him. I could see another figure approaching us slowly.
"He's with me." he said when he noticed me glance behind him over and over.

  As soon as he was in arm's reach, he grabbed my arms and handcuffed my wrists together. "Y'all never cared about me." he said as he gave me a shove to make me start walking. "Bullshit Steve!" I snarled at him. "That's bullshit and you know it!" I said as he shoved me again.
  The other guy didn't intervene, he just stood back and watched us go back and forth. I couldn't

believe my ears as he explained why he did all of this begin with. People are dead or about to die because of jealousy. I shook my head as Steve forced me inside of a dark green jeep. As I got situated in the back seat, I began to wonder how long it was sitting here. "I gotta pay more attention." I thought to myself as I shook my head.

  Steve drove through the iron gates and up to the biggest house I had ever seen in my life. "Beautiful right?" Steve asked as he watched my facial expression through the rearview mirror. I couldn't believe he was making small talk like I wasn't handcuffed and held against my will. I rolled my eyes and released a frustrated sigh.
  "I can't believe they let you out alone. I've been watching you since you first got here and I expected to see one of them." Steve said to me as he parked the jeep.
He stepped out and snatched my out roughly by my arm. We both toppled over onto the ground.
"Bitch ass nigga." I said under my breath.
"Da fuck you say?!" he screamed at me as he got off the ground.
"Bitch! Ass! Nigga!" I said loud and clear then spit on his shoe.
I expected him to kick me or something but he just stared at me a few seconds then snatched me off the ground. "C'mon!" he screamed in my ear and lead me inside the house.

  The inside of the house was even more beautiful than the outside of it. We got on an elevator and went down to a lower level. "Check her." the other guy said in a weird accent. I almost forgot he was with us before he said that. As Steve began to pat me down roughly, alarm filled my body because I have the tracking device on me. It's the only way the others will be able to find me.

"Well, well, well. Looky here." Steve said as he held up the tracking device for the other guy to see. I watched the guy nod his head and check his watch.

"You got something else?" Steve asked and I shook my head.

He snatched my jacket off my body and I stared at him confused about what the hell he would need my jacket for.

I watched him walk away with the jacket draped over his shoulder as he bent over a chair. It looked like he was putting something together but I couldn't see what it was. I took a step closer to get a better look but the guy blocked my path then my line of vision.

"Hurry. Gotta go." the guy said as I stood there trying to figure out how he got one of Boss Lady's men to turn on her, if he wasn't working with her. I knew he was one of her men because him and Aurel has the same accent.

"Ok, ok." Steve said and walked towards us without my jacket. "Damn I hate to miss this." Steve said and I gave him a questioning look.

He grabbed my arm and lead me back out of the house and into the jeep. This time, the other guy took the wheel and Steve sat in the back with me. "Step one of the mission is complete." Steve said out loud.

"What did you do?" I asked him.

"Just be happy you're with me and not them." he said before he punched me in the ear.

I heard a faint ringing sound. I could feel my body sway from side to side before everything went black.

Alexis

As I listened to Vanessa's mom call her Nessie on the tape, my blood began to boil. I was already pissed that they were treating me like some type of handicapped person or like they secretly thought I couldn't get the job done. Vanessa always has my back and it's about time I start having hers. I climbed in my bed and waited patiently for Phat to leave. I ducked in Chris' room, saw that he was gone and when I made it to the living room, so was Vanessa. "Perfect." I said out loud to myself. I grabbed the last picture and tape recorder and pressed play.
"Well done Baby Girl! The picture you are looking at is of Terrance Thomas. Baby don't get distracted by his dark brown skin and light brown eyes like I did. He can't do anything right girl and he failed at the most important job I've ever given him! Then turned snitch! I've already done most of the work for you so all you have to do is go to the address on the back of the picture and press the red button. When Aurel comes after this last hit to pay you, he will also have directions on how to get to my house which is where we'll meet. $10,000." and the tape ended.

I'm so fucking confused because I don't know if I need a gun or what's going to happen when I get to the address. I walked in Vanessa's room, saw she bought new gadgets and left them on her nightstand. I walked over to it and realized they were tracking devices and two of them were on. There was another one just sitting on the dresser with a remote and tracking device, so I grabbed it and turned it on.

I left the remote on the dresser and slid the device in my pocket. I grabbed the machine gun out of the closet that she didn't know I knew she had and left.

I entered in my destination and set out to kill the last person. About an hour later I pulled up to this sign that said enter here but there was no building. I hopped out of my truck, walked to the sign and saw a little door that looks like the cellar door at my grandma's house. I pulled it open and used my phone as a flashlight to guide my steps. I walked cautiously down the steps until I made it to the floor. I was completely out of breath by this time and had to bend over to catch it. I walked slowly through the spacious room I was in until I got to a pit.

"HELP ME!" a male voice screamed.
I looked down into the pit and saw the man from the photo inside of it so I started searching for the red button. As soon as I found it, I hit it without a second thought but nothing happened. I walked back over to the pit and saw that four slots opened inside of it and rats were crawling out of each hole. I'd never seen rats this big in my life. I watched him kick them one at a time away from him as they jumped out of the holes faster and faster. He kicked one just as another one bit into his ankle. He kicked it away and fell in the process. I stood there watching as they tore into his flesh.
"Where the fuck she get all of these rats?" I asked myself as I backed away from the pit.

"That was easy. They thought I couldn't help!" I said out loud to myself. I turned around and headed towards the stairs so I could make it home before they got back. If I leave now, even if they

beat me back I can say I just went to the store. When I got to the stairs they shifted. I tried to step on the first step but the staircase started to slide into the wall and the cellar door slammed shut. Fear gripped my soul as I stumbled backwards and fell. I could hear faint squeaking noises and when I turned my phone around to look, I noticed the rats had filled the pit and were now using each other to climb out.

Vanessa

I pulled up to the house and strangely there was no black van parked out front. I climbed out of the car, wondering why Aurel hadn't showed up with my payment. By the time I got to the door, Chris and Phat pulled into the yard and that's when I realized Alexis' truck was gone. Panic and fear ripped through my body as I high tailed it through the house looking for Alexis. This felt like Deja vu! I ran back into the living room just as Phat and Chris walked in the house.

"The hell wrong with you now?" Chris asked.
"Alexis is gone." I said as I ran to the box but it was empty. I turned around with tears streaming down my face and looked at Phat. "You let her do a hit?" I asked with a lump in my throat. I didn't give him time to answer as I ran back into their room to find the picture and tape recorder.

The picture was gone but she left the recorder so I grabbed it and ran back into the living room. We listened to it but it didn't help us at all without having the picture because the address is on it.

"Fuck!" I screamed as I threw the tape recorder against the wall and watched it shatter into pieces and land on the floor.

A loud wail came out of my body as I dropped down to the floor. She's my best friend, the only person that understands me and accepts me and now she's gone because of me. The tape clearly says that after the job is complete Aurel will show up with money and an address, but he hasn't even showed up to pay us for the ones we just did. The last hit was a setup and since we all completed those hits at the same time he didn't come at all.

"Where you going?" Phat asked because I stood to my feet and walked away.

"I need a minute." I tossed over my shoulder as I headed into my room.

As soon as I opened the door I saw paper on my bed that I didn't leave there, two remotes on my nightstand and one on my dresser. The one on my dresser was closer so I picked it up but it lost signal. I grabbed my bag and slid it inside of it. I walked over to my nightstand and noticed one of them was labeled with an A and the other with a B but they were both in the same place. I threw B in my bag and made my way to my bed to read the letter:

Hey V,

So look don't be mad at me, but I went and bought three tracking devices. I don't know why I bought three when I only needed two but something told me to get it so I did. If you're reading this, I got caught and if you guys can't save me don't blame yourself. I take full responsibility and I love you all. Any who, Tracking device A is in my pocket and B is taped under one of those Black Vans that I'm following back to Boss Lady's house.

Frankie
p.s. Come save me

As soon as I read the first sentence all of my tears dried up. It's time out for the crybaby shit, simply because my sisters are missing and these tears ain't gone find them. I checked my bag to make sure all of my knives and grenades were in place. I slid out of my cute clothes and threw on an all-black jogging suit and Ashiko boots. I grabbed my bag and headed out to the living room.

"Damn Rambo!" Chris said failing miserably at making light of the situation.

"Let's go." I said after I made sure the remote still had the tracking devices' signal.

"Where we headed?" Phat asked after we loaded up and pulled off. I told them what Frankie said in her letter.

"Maybe Lexi got the other one." Chris said.

"I hope so since Frankie didn't take it but the remote doesn't have a signal on it." I said as I continued to drive to our destination.

I was driving like a bat out of hell and it only took 30 minutes before I passed the bumpy road that I was supposed to turn on. I drove up a few more feet, hit a U-turn and turned on the road.

I drove down the bumpy road and slowed down when I saw headlights. "That's Frankie's car." I said as I threw my car in park and hopped out.

Chris and Phat followed suit as I looked around the inside for any type of struggle but there wasn't one. We hopped back in the car and continued to drive until we came to a gate. I could see guard towers but I didn't see any guards. Chris got out of the car and walked up to the gate and pushed it slightly because it was ajar. It rocked but didn't open completely. "C'mon." I yelled out of the window.

When he hopped in the car, I backed up to get a good distance before I rammed the gates and drove the rest of the way to the house. We all hopped out and made our way into the house. I pushed the door open and the sight before me made my mouth drop. It was empty. There wasn't a piece of furniture in sight. I checked the remote and I hadn't reached the tracking device so maybe Frankie is still here.

"Aye let's check down there." I said when I noticed the elevator.

My gut was telling me not to go but I had to be sure she wasn't down there. We loaded onto the elevator that only went down and I could hear the tracking device ticking.

"I didn't know these things tick when you get closer to them." I said as I followed the noise. "What the fuck?" I said when I saw a chair facing the opposite direction with a note on top of Frankie's jacket.

"You did all of that to kill me but I ended up killing you"

"That's all it says." I shrugged after reading the note out loud. I looked at Chris and Phat and they looked as clueless as I felt. I grabbed Frankie's jacket and my heart got caught in my throat. I took a cautious step back as I peered at the bomb tied down to the chair in front of me that timed us perfectly. 10, 9, 8, 7, 6.......

Chris

I didn't know what the fuck was going on. All I know is what I heard and what I heard sounded like a fucking bomb. I think Phat and Vanessa are both shocked because they are slowly backing away from it. I looked past Vanessa and saw we had five seconds to get the fuck out of dodge. Considering it may take five seconds for the elevator doors to open we may be doomed. Not to mention trapped since I don't think the elevator will work after an explosion.
"Fuck this." I said out loud as I snatched Vanessa up.
When I swung her around, her feet hit Phat and knocked him out of the trance he was in. We hauled ass to other side of this floor and ran in a room. I slammed the door closed and covered my ears. I sat crouched down with my body covering Vanessa's for about thirty seconds.
What the fuck?" Phat asked as he slowly stood to his feet. He walked cautiously to the door after nothing happened.
"Man where you goin?" I asked as I tried to grab him.
"Shit I'm tryna see what's going on?" he said and opened the door. I shook my head and closed it back behind them and continued to hover over Vanessa.
"Aye Chris c'mere!" Phat yelled from the other room.
"Man hell naw!" I yelled back with a frown.

I ain't trying to get blown the fuck up fucking with Phat's curious ass. Vanessa crawled away from me and had this faraway look in her eyes.
"Nessa." I said as I inched closer to her. She continued to look off as if in deep thought then she got up and walked out of the room. "These mu'fuckers must have a death wish or something." I said to myself as I stood to my feet and walked out of the door. I looked around cautiously and pushed the elevator button as soon as I got to it. The goal for me is to get out of dodge before the fucking bomb realizes that it didn't go off.

     I glanced to my left and saw Vanessa and Phat were standing directly in front of the chair. "Really man? What are y'all the bomb squad or something?" I asked getting pissed off.
I wanted to just get in the elevator and leave but if something happened to them and I survived because I left them, I don't think I could handle that. We've already lost Frankie and Alexis, even though it was their doing for running off and going all commando on us; but I can't lose the only family I have left.

     Out of nowhere, Vanessa cracked up with laughter. I mean this girl done bent all over laughing. Phat looked at her then back at me before he shrugged his shoulders then turned back around. "Steve's a dummy! He got us though." Vanessa said as she caught her breath and continued to examine the bomb before her. I was beyond confused and had no idea what she would find funny at this very moment.
"Care to explain?" I asked as I walked up to her to stand on the other side of her.
"So check this out.... being in my room a lot alone left me a lot of time to research things I may have

wanted to do later." she said then gestured towards the bomb.

"You wanted to build a bomb?" Phat asked as he looked at her with a side eye.

I chuckled softly because this crazy ass girl never ceases to amaze me. I don't know what she doesn't know and it's amazing because she taught herself.

"Did you forget I like killing people? I mean how easy would it be to get everybody that I need gone in one room and blow them up? Cool right?" she asked as she looked back and forth between us. We both just looked at her little psychotic ass.

"Man I hope she change when we start having babies." I thought to myself. I bet you're like "Y'all ain't even together" but we are. Have been since she called me and said she's ready.

If we make it out of this alive, she may ask me to marry her once she sees her surprise that I have waiting for her.

"So what's funny?" Phat asked and I could tell he was still confused.

"The dummy didn't connect the timer to the bomb!" she said in a matter of fact tone like we were supposed to know what the hell she was talking about. "Ugh! In order for the bomb to go off without a detonator, he would have had to successfully connected the timer to it." she said and rolled her eyes at us.

"All I want to know is if it's active right now. Fuck all that other shit." I said and her eyes got big.

"Oh shit, yeah it's active!" she yelled on her way to the elevator.

We followed suit, hopped on and rode it back up to the floor we were on. We walked around the entire estate and it took every bit of two hours and man I was dog tired when we left, no closer to finding Frankie or Alexis than we were when we arrived.

Phat

I drove us back to the house and silently thanked God for sparing us. Even if it was just a technicality, it was still a blessing to me. I was hoping Boss Lady would make a phone call or leave us a package or something, but three days went by and we still had nothing. I had been combing the streets looking for Alexis, but I kept coming up empty. Vanessa wasn't any help and I don't know why. It's like she's always somewhere else even though she's physically here. She hasn't gone out a single time to look for Frankie or Alexis and that's strange because I know she goes hard for them both.

Every time I see her, she has the remotes to the remaining two tracking devices next to her and her laptop. She hasn't even been out to kill anyone. I think killing people calms her like smoking weed calms a smoker because since she hasn't been killing anyone, her attitude is a force to be reckoned with. Hell she won't even communicate with Chris. She just stays in her room and every time I check on her she's on her laptop but she won't say what she's doing.

I haven't been to sleep in these three days either. I mean, how can a man sleep peacefully knowing the love of his life is somewhere possibly in pain while pregnant with his child.

"Aye, lemme holla at you." Chris stated from the doorway just as my cell phone started to ring.

I signaled for him to give me a moment because the call came from a number that I don't have saved in my phone.

"Yeah?" I answered as I looked up at Chris. I waved him in and he sat in the chair next to the bed.
"The baby need some diapers." I heard a voice say over the phone. I pulled the phone away from my ear with a frown on my face.
"Who is this?" I asked with aggravation evident in my voice.
"Brittany!" she answered with an attitude. I frowned my face up even more because the bitch is calling me on some pure fuckery!
"Bitch the baby ain't even here yet!" I snapped at her.
"Junior will need some when he gets here. I wanna see you." she cooed into the phone.
"Man don't call me no fuckin mo' 'til you in labor. I want a DNA test and if it's mine I'll buy some diapers!" I snapped then hung up the phone in her face.
I threw the phone on the bed and let out an exasperated sigh.

My phone started to ring again and Chris shook his head at me. He grabbed the phone and tossed it to me and it was her again. I silenced the phone and sat it down in my lap.
"What's up?" I asked Chris as it started to ring again. He waited for me to power the phone off.
"We gotta figure out how to get Vanessa out this funk man so we can find Frankie and Alexis." Chris said to me.
I could see the worry lines all over his face as he stared at me and waited on my response. I caught a glimpse of something at the door and when I turned my head it was Vanessa. She stood in my doorway silent and as still as a royal guard all the while shooting daggers at me. My heart started to race and

not because I was scared of her but because I didn't know how long she had been standing there and I didn't want her to tell Alexis anything prematurely.

I stared at her as I waited for her to throw a knife or one those stars she has or something, because it's clear that she's upset about something. Chris followed my line of vision until his eyes fell upon Vanessa. I watched him look back and forth between us for a few seconds, like he was waiting on one of us to say something. I don't know why she's not talking, but the guilt of what I think she may have heard is stopping me from speaking up.

"What's up?" Chris asked as he continued to look between us. I shrugged my shoulders because I didn't want to give something away.

"What's up Nessa?" I asked as she continued to stare at me. *"This bitch is a fucking lunatic!"* I thought to myself.

It took a minute or so but she finally broke the stare and focused her attention on Chris. Then she walked away.

"Your girl crazy man." I said to Chris as I shook my head.

"Shit she probably heard your conversation and is about to kill you when she come back in here." Chris said followed by loud laughter.

I stared at him trying to figure out what the hell was so funny.

It may have been funny if we were talking about an ordinary chick, but Vanessa is about as far away from ordinary as it can get. He's sitting here joking about someone that enjoys killing, killing me. Shit I'll never forget when she told me if I hurt Alexis again that Alexis won't be able to stop her from killing me. I believed her then and I hope like hell she didn't hear any of that conversation.

Vanessa

I have been working my butt off these last couple of days trying to figure out everything I could about these damn tracking devices that Frankie bought. It took a couple of days but I'm finally on to something. I wish I could call my dad to get his help with finding Frankie and Alexis, but I'm still not sure if he's a friend or foe.

Finding Alexis is a no brainer, it's a must that I find my best friend. I called the Doctor's office and rescheduled her doctor's appointment for her so she when I bring her home we can check on the baby.

I was so excited about the progress I was making and I wanted to tell the guys about it because I know they've been worried about me. Imagine my surprise when I walked up to the door and heard Phat going off on somebody. I heard the entire conversation and me being pissed was an understatement. I stood in the doorway and gave him a stare, wishing like hell the way I was looking could kill him. I was even more mad at myself for not having any stars or knives in reach. I made a mental note to place them around the house strategically when I have time and nobody is around. You know for just in case purposes.

Phat stared at me and I could see the sweat on his forehead. His nervousness radiated off of his skin and as crazy as it may sound, I could smell the fear. See, fear saves us in a lot of situations but it gives us away in others. Say for instance, it's not the dark that we are afraid of, it's the not knowing what's in the dark. Our fear allows us to sense when something is off and we become more alert and are able to protect ourselves in some cases. In instances like this or when you're near a pit bull, your fear gives you away because dogs can sense fear. Not saying I'm an animal or anything like that, I'm just saying.

  I stood there and stared Phat down trying to figure out if I should kill him now or wait until later. After weighing my options, I decided he's more useful to the search alive, plus I don't want Lexi to come back mad at me. I'm going to tell her what I heard and let her decide if she wants him alive or dead, and handle that for her. I guess it's not really my place to just kill him anyway. Not to mention I have no idea who he was talking to. *"If I figure that out and kill him then that will dead the whole situation."* I thought to myself as I turned to head back to my room.
  As soon as I made it through my door I started to have second thoughts about what I was planning to do. Sure I could find a way to get Phat's phone records to figure out who the girl was. Sure I could go to her house and kill her but she's pregnant and that child didn't ask to be made. So, Phat better hope and pray that the child ain't his.

  I grabbed my laptop and the tracking devices then headed back to Phat's room.
"Can we talk in the living room?" I asked then walked away.
It was my way of letting them know that it wasn't up for debate. I did not want to be in the room Phat's shares with Alexis while she's gone. I don't want to think about the fact that she's not here. I don't want to think about what she's going through,

if they're hurting her or feeding her. I need my focus to be on finding her.

      I took a seat on the couch and pulled my research up so I could glance back at it if I needed to while I explain it to them. It took them a few minutes to come in the living room and Chris walked in first, but I'm no dummy. I know Phat doesn't know if I heard the conversation or not and I'm not going to say anything about it. He let Chris come in first just in case I was going to throw something.

"So check this out." I began and stopped because they both stayed away from me. I frowned my face up at them before I shook my head and continued. "I figured out where Frankie got the tracking devices. I called and they told me the instructions on how to use them were online. It took me a minute to figure it out but I've got it." I said and could see Phat's eyes light up.

"What more do you need to know how to do?" Chris asked.

I can tell he was thinking about it the same way I was. See, I thought I just hold this transceiver and go towards the red dot on the screen. It's only that simple when there is a signal.

"I bet you didn't know that I can email myself the last set of coordinates before it lost signal did you?" I asked with a smirk on my face.

I was already dressed so I just needed them to get ready so we could go get my girl.

TRUE GLORY PUBLICATIONS

IF YOU WOULD LIKE TO BE A PART OF OUR TEAM, PLEASE SEND YOUR SUBMISSIONS BY EMAIL TO TRUEGLORYPUBLICATIONS@GMAIL.COM. PLEASE INCLUDE A BRIEF BIO, A SYNOPSIS OF THE BOOK, AND THE FIRST THREE CHAPTERS. SUBMIT USING MICROSOFT WORD WITH FONT IN 11 TIMES NEW ROMAN.

Check out these other great books from True Glory Publications

Twisted Faith of a Side Bitch: Virginia

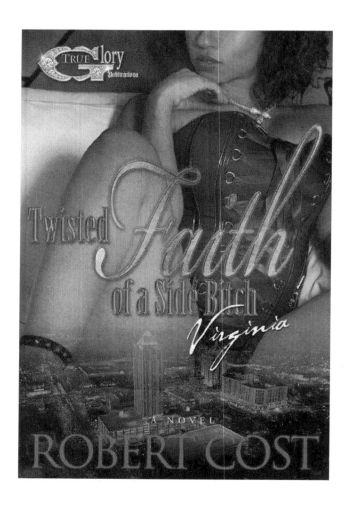

The Wrong Bitch

A Child of a Crackhead Series

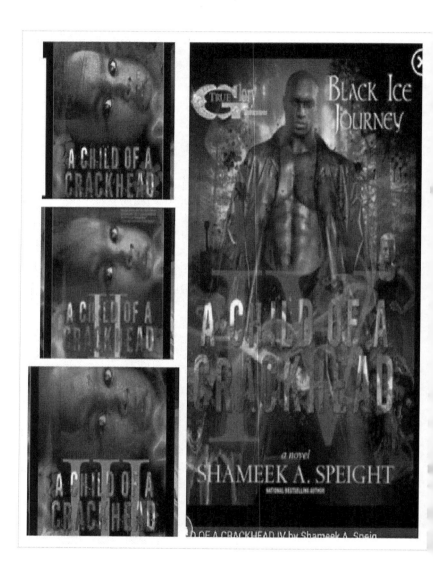

My Husband, Another Woman's Sex Toy

Made in the USA
San Bernardino, CA
02 July 2016